HACKER CHRISTMAS

WHITE HAT SECURITY, BOOK 6

LINZI BAXTER

LINZI BAXTER

Hacker Christmas
White Hat Security Series, Book 6
Copyright © 2018 by Linzi Baxter
Kindle Edition
Cover Artist: Cassy Roop, Pink Ink Designs
Edited by: Red Adept Editing

All rights reserved. Except for use in any review, the reproduction or utilization of this work, in whole or in part, in any form by any electronic, mechanical, or other means now known or hereafter invented, is forbidden without permission of the author.

The unauthorized reproduction or distribution of this copyrighted work is illegal. Criminal copyright infringement (including infringement without monetary gain) is investigated by the FBI and is punishable by up to five years in federal prison and a fine of $250,000.

Please purchase only authorized electronic editions and do not participate in or encourage the electronic piracy of copyrighted materials. Your support of the author's rights is appreciated.

This is a work of fiction. Names, characters, businesses, places, events, and incidents are either the products of the author's imagination or used in a fictitious manner. Any resemblance to actual persons, living or dead, or actual events is purely coincidental.

BLURB

A dark past. A seductive temptation. A hidden secret.

Daisy wants nothing more than to put her past behind her and finally move on, but she can't. After Aaron arranges for her and Neal to fly to California for a romantic vacation, her stress hits a critical high, and in order to clear her mind, she does something unthinkable with someone she doesn't know. Despite being forgiven, Daisy's choice puts her life in danger and she realizes that in order for her to finally move on, she needs to confront her past. More importantly, she needs to forgive herself.

Aaron Ross has Hollywood at his feet and the world in his hands. Instead of enjoying every minute of it, he's counting the seconds until he can retreat from the limelight and finally settle down with Daisy and Neal.

Neal Cross is lying to himself and to the two most important people in his life. He may know everything there is to know about computers and hacking but he has no idea about matters of the heart - except when it comes to Aaron and Daisy.

The three plan a trip to California - and it can't come soon enough. On their trip, all three must make an important choice: do they finally leave their past behind or do they lose the ones they love? Do they leave behind everything they know for something they want, or do they play it safe and stay where they are? Do they face their fears, or do they lose it all?

AUTHOR'S NOTE

White Hat Security Series

Hacker Exposed
    Royal Hacker
    Misunderstood Hacker
    Undercover Hacker
    Hacker Revelation
    Hacker Christmas

Montana Gold (Brotherhood Kindle World)

    Grayson's Angel
    Noah's Love
    Bryson's Treasure - 2019

A Flipping Love Story (Badge of Honor World)

Unlocking Dreams
Unlocking Hope - 2019

Visit linzibaxter.com for more information and release dates.
Join Linzi Baxter Newsletter at Newsletter

PROLOGUE - DAISY

The cold metal flaked as I carved another line on the cage floor. Most people wanted to celebrate a ten-year anniversary. The only thing I wanted was to curl up and die. I recounted the tick marks on the cage floor: three thousand six hundred and fifty ticks. I had been held captive for over ten years. There were days when I was unconscious, so I didn't add a tick. But I had enough ticks to mark my ten-year anniversary of living in hell.

Heels clicked on the wooden staircase—it was the woman in charge of the house. The bitch had an evil streak that rivaled my master's. My bare butt slid across the cold metal floor of my cage until my back hit the iron bars. The cage stood four feet high and four feet wide. The only kind gesture I had seen in ten years was that the temperature of the room was comfortable. Master didn't allow clothes, and I couldn't remember what it felt like to have fabric hug my skin.

Regina Ward, the house manager, flicked the light switch, and I squinted when the dungeon was illuminated. The room didn't remind me of the BDSM clubs I used to visit in Los Angeles. It reminded me of a torture chamber from the latest serial-killer movie. Well, let's be real—I'd been in a cage for ten years, and the last movie I saw was *Ocean's Eleven*.

The sound of Regina's heels hitting the cement made me swivel my head away from the wall of knives. Regina was in her late thirties, and she had black hair that she always wore twisted in a bun. She always wore a pencil skirt and white blouse. If I had to make a guess, the master told her what to wear. In all of my years being locked up, Regina was the only woman I had seen in Master's house who wasn't in a cage.

Her lips twisted into an evil grin as she stepped closer to the cage. "Master wants you clean for a party tonight." No wonder the lady had an evil grin. She enjoyed my screams when Master tortured me. His parties were the worst. They meant I would be everyone's play toy for hours. Each man would show up with a mask on—I'd never seen anyone's face. I only hoped the man who wore the Kennedy mask wouldn't show.

The man who wore the Kennedy mask enjoyed the sight of my blood. After everyone finished using me as their toy, he would spend the rest of the night whipping my body until blood coated the floor and I passed out from the pain. It would then take weeks for my body to heal. Master hadn't allowed me to be beaten so badly when I was his only pet. Last week, I witnessed his latest kidnapping victim get beaten to death when she tried to escape. Over the years, many women had passed through the dungeon. I would tell them how to stay alive, but they never listened.

Regina opened the cage door. I had no choice but to crawl out, or she would use the cattle prod on my bare skin. As I exited the cage, she tapped the toe of her red high heel on the floor. Everything I needed was in the dungeon—in ten years, I saw the sun twice, when Master had a party outside. They fed me in there. My bathroom was in there.

"You have an hour to get ready and eat." The witch turned on her heel and went back up the stairs. After she shut the door, I heard the audible click of the steel bar locking in place.

I let out a breath. Sometimes, she enjoyed hitting me for no reason. When I tried to defend myself, she would tell Master, and I would spend hours under his whip. The longer I stayed under his care, the more I wanted to end my own life. In ten years, nobody had found me. *Can I make it any longer, waiting for someone to find me? Nope, tonight is my last night. I will offend one of his friends and make sure he kills me. I can't take it any longer.*

The shower felt good as the water ran over my body. Once I finished cleaning my body, I lay down on the couch in the dungeon and tried to formulate a plan. *Tonight is the night.* I couldn't take the pain any longer, and I thought no one would still be looking for me.

Missy, the woman who Master killed last week, swore that her father would never stop the search to find her and that we would be free. She was the first kidnapping victim to give me hope, at least until I watched Master beat her until the life went out of her eyes.

I had lost track of time. I heard the loud steps come down the stairs. What surprised me was that it was only one set. Normally, Master had a few friends come down when he had a party. I hurried off the couch and presented myself on my knees. If I wanted him to be mad, I needed to disobey in front of his friends.

The concrete hurt my knees as I kneeled and twined my hands behind my back. I cast my eyes to the floor. I could see Master's expensive leather shoes as he stepped in front of me. Master was in his late sixties and was one of the most powerful executives in Hollywood. We had met at an after-party following a movie premiere. I had been Annabella Axson's hairdresser—she was the lead actress for a summer blockbuster, and she had given me a ticket to the party. Generally, I would say no, but the latest tabloid said my Hollywood crush, Aaron Ross, would be there. He was one of the highest-paid actors and a very nice man. Annabella said she had seen him many times at the local BDSM clubs with beautiful subs. I knew I didn't have a chance at catching his eye, but he was so nice to look at.

The party was in full swing when I showed up, and I was at the bar when Master came up and asked me if I wanted a drink. I knew him for breaking and making careers. I figured I had to say yes to the drink. The sweet taste of Moscato wine was the last thing I remembered about that night. When I woke, I was in the cage.

A kick to one leg brought me out of my walk

down memory lane. "Are you not listening, my pet?" Master growled.

"Yes, Master."

"I asked if you are ready to have fun."

"Yes, Master." I was going to stick to my plan to disobey in front of his friends.

He reached down and wrapped his hands through my long blond hair. My hair was naturally brown, but Master didn't like brown, so Regina came down to the dungeon once a month to dye my hair. When he yanked my hair upward, my only option was to follow. Once I was standing in front of him, he leaned in and whispered in my ear, "You will have a night to remember." Something in his voice sent shivers down my spine, and not the good shivers. His voice held no remorse. He was evil to the core.

It seemed we had the same idea. We were both done—I no longer wanted to live, and he no longer wanted me. He pushed me toward the stairs. Slight excitement went through me. *I might get to see the sun before I die.* I only hoped to see daylight. It had been years. My legs, weak from years of malnutrition, hurt as I climbed the stairs, I stumbled when I heard a cry. It looked as though my replacement had arrived.

As I opened the door, my only wish came true.

Sunlight poured in through the windows of Master's mansion. I couldn't help but stop and relish the sunlight and the sight of birds flying around outside. I didn't care if the bright light hurt my eyes. It was the closest I'd been to freedom in years. I could have used the opportunity to run. The most he would have done was kill me, and I had gotten to a point where I didn't want to live any longer.

Master became irritated and pushed me from behind. I stumbled forward and caught myself against the dining room table. When I looked to the left, I saw the new girl, who couldn't have been any older than twenty, tied to a Saint Andrew's cross. Another cross, which I assumed would be my place, stood next to her. When I turned to head toward the cross, Master pulled me by the hair. "Go to the kitchen," he growled.

I turned and walked in the opposite direction of the crying girl. No matter how many times I'd seen the women Master brought home cry until he beat the life out of them, it still affected me, and I wept on the inside. In the kitchen sat a plate with a steak, mashed potatoes, and a glass of wine. It was all I needed to see. Either Master planned to kill me or give me away, but I knew it would be my last night.

"Eat," he told me before he turned on a heel and walked away.

He didn't want me to answer, so I stayed quiet. I sat down at the counter and looked around the beautiful home owned by a man who had more money than he knew what to do with and spent his time killing women for pleasure.

The kitchen had a set of French doors. If I could get to them unnoticed, I might be able to outrun the dogs. I had heard the last girl's screams as the dogs tore through her body. Master had shown me her remains, so I knew what would happen if I ran.

The steak melted on my tongue—I had forgotten what it tasted like. The wine went down with ease. It wasn't until I finished eating that I noticed I didn't feel right. *Is this how it will end? Did he poison my last meal?*

When he walked back into the room, his words were hard to understand: "Looks like it's taking effect. This will be fun."

He led me from the kitchen into the living room and strapped me to the second cross. As I had eaten the steak, his friends had arrived. Four men sat on the couches, with different presidential masks on. I let out a sigh of relief when I didn't see the Kennedy mask. Master walked up and ran his hand down my face. "Well, men, I've had this one for ten years. The highest bidder takes her home." I suddenly understood the drugs. They would make it easier to transport me.

"Each of you will have a go at her, and then the bidding will start."

I tried to focus on the four men, but it was hard. It seemed as though the man in the middle tensed when master spoke. His body language suggested that he wanted to be anywhere else.

The man on the left was the first to jump up and grab a whip. Master stepped back and picked up his scotch. The first strike hurt, even with the drugs. These men didn't warm the body up—their main goal was pure sadism. Using the technique I'd been using for years, I zoned out and pictured Aaron Ross gently whipping his subs.

When the sadist with the whip stopped, I focused on the next man. It worried me that he seemed so tense. He stepped up so close that I could feel his body heat against me. He slowly dragged his hand down my face and leaned into my ear.

"Step back."

"Don't snap at me. If I'm going to pay millions for something, I will look carefully."

The guy didn't back down from my master at all.

He leaned back in. "I'm sorry I have to do this, but you will be safe by tonight."

Before I could blink, he stepped back. *What does he mean, 'safety?'* He would just be another master keeping me under his foot. I didn't plan on letting that happen. Once we stepped outside tonight, I would run for my life.

I watched as he gripped the whip in his hand. It made a loud sound when he cracked it, but it stunned me when I barely felt it against me—his touch was featherlike. It was how I remembered it from long ago. Then he went again, a little harder. Even though it sounded and looked like it should've hurt, it didn't. I was almost in a place of pure bliss when the woman next to me screamed. I looked over to find that Master had taken a whip to her. Blood ran down her right breast, tears streamed from her dark-brown eyes, and her red lips quivered.

"I will buy her for five million. Take my offer now or take it off the table," the man who just whipped me said.

The room became quiet. My master looked him up and down, and something passed over his face. "She is no longer for sale." *There goes my chance to run.*

The other two men stood still in the room. The

man who just whipped me straightened his posture. I bet if I saw his face, I would see pure hatred. "You're telling me I flew in to buy a slave that you will no longer sell?"

"You can have this one for your troubles."

The man cocked his head to the side. "I think I want both."

Master charged at him when he got within a foot of the other man. The man with the whip punched my master, and he dropped to the ground like a dead weight. Regina came running into the room with a gun. She shook as she pointed it at the three men. "Out."

"Not until I get what I came for." *This man is dangerous.* I didn't know who I wanted to stay with. He seemed deadly—I'd never seen anyone take down Master or even try to. What Master would do to them scared most people.

Sirens rang in the distance. I couldn't tell if it was all part of the drugs playing out in my head or if the man would save me. Regina stepped forward a second too late. A large man dressed in black stepped up behind her and disarmed her. While I watched in awe, the two men beside me grunted as two more men I had never seen dressed in black took down the other people here to bid on me. The man who'd whipped me took off his mask. He was breathtaking. "Ma'am, my name is Sam, and we are taking you home."

"Home?" *Where is home? I've been here for so many years.*

One of his friends took the woman next to me down and wrapped her in a blanket.

Sam undid my arms, and I collapsed into him. "Please kill me," I begged. "I can't do this any longer."

"How long have you been here?" His deep voice soothed me.

"Ten years."

Sam let out a stream of cuss words. Master stirred on the floor. Before I had time to run, Sam pulled a gun from his waistband and shot him in the head. "Now, you don't have to worry."

"But you will make me your slave. It will never end."

"No, you are going home."

"I have no home," I whispered as the drugs took over my body.

1
DAISY

Five years later

"Daisy, let's discuss what took place last night," Dr. Robison said.

Leave it to a therapist to get straight to the objective. My ass had barely touched the white sofa before the words escaped her mouth. I knew that neither Aaron nor Neal, my doms, told her about the night before. When Brock, my boss and devoted friend, escorted me toward his apartment, I saw Mistress Rubie's strained smile. It wasn't fair that my therapist was part of my life outside her office. It didn't give me the chance to avoid things.

"No."

"This is a safe place, and you know I won't repeat anything you say inside this room. Let's talk about how you did a BDSM scene with a new dom, with neither of your doms at the club last night. Did Aaron and Neal know you planned to go to the club?"

I didn't want to talk about it because I didn't understand why I asked a stranger to scene with me. Before I left Blackwood Security, Aaron called to invite me to California for Christmas. The conversation should have made me excited, but instead dread filled my mind, and I wanted my mind to go blank after the call. I would have asked Neal to scene, but he had flown to Washington to have dinner with the president of the United States. Neal had asked me to go to DC, but I stayed in Ft. Lauderdale to work. The only thing I could think to clear my mind was a scene, so instead of asking Brock, as I should've, I asked the first dom I ran into.

My mind wandered to the men I cared most about. I didn't know what I would do when they left me, which I knew they would. Neal ran an elite cyber-security company, Black Hat, and Aaron was a top Hollywood actor. Being public about a three-way relationship wasn't an option for either of them. So instead of waiting for them to dump me, I think I chose to do the scene so they would leave me, which would have been easier for them than leaving me for my past. Nobody wanted somebody who talked about herself in the third person as his wife.

I contemplated not telling Dr. Robison why, but over the years, she had figured out my stall tactics. She had moved my sessions to the end of the day so she could keep me in her office until I talked. "Daisy thinks it would be easier if they dumped her."

Dr. Robison tapped her pen on the notebook in front of her. I never wanted to see what she wrote in her notebook about me. "Do you no longer like Neal and Aaron? I know it's hard with Aaron gone a lot, but do you still want to be with them?"

I loved them more than anything. But if I continued to be with them, I didn't think I could recover when they broke my heart by letting me go. "They won't be with Daisy permanently. Daisy's fallen too hard already. Daisy doesn't think she can recover when they move on. Neither of them can keep Daisy in their lives. Aaron is a top Hollywood actor, and Neal is the CEO of Black Hat. He could lose clients." Even though Dr. Robison's office walls were a soothing gray and the lights were soft, the room felt dark and cold as I talked about breaking up with Neal and Aaron.

"Have you talked about your feelings with Neal

and Aaron? What triggered you to pick a random dom last night?"

I pulled the drawstring on my black yoga pants. "No. Daisy doesn't want to bother them with her issues. They will get rid of Daisy faster. Aaron wants Daisy to come to California next week."

Dr. Robison left her chair and sat next to me on the couch. She grabbed my hand. "Daisy, I'm talking to you as your friend, not your therapist. You've lived with Neal for almost a year, and Aaron has been with you guys for three months. Have they given you any reason to believe they don't want to be with you?" When I didn't answer, she continued. "They both look at you like you are their everything. Do they know this will be your first time back to California since Sam saved you?"

The thought of setting foot on California soil made my hands sweat. "They can't be with me forever. It's been five years. I should be able to go to California again."

"Don't downplay how you feel about California. Why can't you be with them for forever?"

I reached up and wiped my eyes then admitted something I held close since Neal and I got together—it was the reason we couldn't be together forever. "Daisy's damaged," I whispered.

Dr. Robison pulled me into a hug, and I felt her wet tears on my neck. "You're perfect, Daisy. You've been through something most people wouldn't survive. You lived with an evil man for ten years."

"Master said he made it so Daisy can't have children. Daisy also can't stop talking in third person, even though she tries." I chastised myself for calling him Master. I worked every day not to call the man from my nightmares Master.

Dr. Robison's body tensed at my words. "First of all, he is not your master. Secondly, have you gone to see a doctor and asked if something's wrong?"

It had been five years since Sam Blackwood saved me from a life of captivity on the day I planned to kill myself. I still hadn't asked a doctor if I could have kids. Why would it matter? Nobody would ever want to marry someone held captive for years. "No."

"How about we find out for sure before you say you're damaged. Even if you can't have kids, you can adopt. I never want to hear you call yourself damaged. You're a strong, brave woman. Emotional issues such as worrying about having kids are things you need to discuss with your doms. You need to sit them down and have a lengthy conversation. When is Aaron coming back?"

I loved Neal with all my heart, but when Aaron

was in California, life felt off. "Neal and I are to fly out next week. But Neal won't want Daisy anymore after what happened last night."

Dr. Robison released me from the hug. "Let's talk about why Neal doesn't want to be with you anymore."

"Brock called him last night and told him Daisy went to Club Sanctorum and scened. Brock told Neal he had to break up the scene because Daisy had blood running down her back. Neal didn't want to talk to Daisy after his conversation with Brock. He told Brock to take care of Daisy and said he would be back tonight. Daisy stayed at Brock's last night, and even Brock could barely say a word."

Brock had been by my side since Sam carried me out of the evil bastard's house. He held me while we flew to Ft. Lauderdale, and I lived with him for the first couple of years. Brock was like my brother, and last night he couldn't look at me. I hadn't only wrecked my relationship with Neal and Aaron. Today at work, he didn't even come to the front to talk to me at reception. Every day since I started at Blackwood Security, he'd come up front and chat. I could hardly hold back the tears at work. When the alarm rang to remind me of my appointment, I rushed out of the building. I didn't even know if I would have a job the next day.

Dr. Robison's words broke my train of thought. "Let's not jump to conclusions. Talk to Neal tonight. Did you do the scene last night because you want Neal and Aaron to leave you? Or was it about your trip to California?"

She had a good point. After Aaron's call, my world seemed to tilt. I couldn't get my brain to turn off. So I asked someone I had seen before to do a scene. "Daisy might've done the scene because of stress. When he whipped me, Daisy went back to her old master's house in her head. Daisy couldn't speak. She zoned out. Daisy didn't even feel the whip as it hit her skin. It wasn't until Brock screamed something and released her from the cross that Daisy realized how far she had let it go."

My phone vibrated next to me. Deep down, I hoped it was Neal or Aaron, but I figured it was Jessica. I looked at the screen to find a text from Neal. *Brock will pick you up from therapy and bring you to the penthouse.* My stomach turned at his words. *Will tonight be my last chance to see Neal? Will Aaron ever say goodbye?* I couldn't help it. Tears appeared in my eyes.

"Don't jump to conclusions, Daisy. You need to

talk to Neal. Don't think you know what he will say. You need to sit down and talk to them about California. Those men can't read your mind. Have you ever talked about what happened, or has everyone glazed over it? You need to talk about it, or your relationship with these men won't go anywhere."

The loud knock on the door startled me. "Come in," Dr. Robison yelled. The door creaked open, and Brock stuck his head in.

"Hey, Daisy, I'll be in the lobby when you finish. Don't hurry." When Dr. Robison nodded, Brock stepped back and closed the door.

Dr. Robison gripped my hand. "I care about you deeply, Daisy. I want you to be happy, and I think Neal and Aaron can do that. But you need to open a line of communication, or this relationship will fail. Not because of your past, but because you are keeping things from Aaron and Neal. Men can't read your mind, and you know in this lifestyle how important communication is. If you need me in the next two weeks, call."

"Can you help Daisy with something before Daisy goes?"

Dr. Robsion shifted in her seat. "I would help you with anything."

"How can Daisy stop talking in third person?

She manages it sometimes but not always."

"There are three big reasons people speak in third person. It's because they are narcissistic, self-obsessed, or detached from reality. From years of sitting with you, it's clear to me that you use it to stay detached from reality. Think about what you say before you say it, and try to speak in first person if you are ready. I think you've been ready for a while."

She was right. I used it to stay detached, but I wanted to show Neal and Aaron that I was trying.

I took a deep breath. "I'll try."

Dr. Robison wrapped her arms around me. I hugged her goodbye then walked toward the door to face my friend—at least I hoped he was still my friend. When I opened the door, he looked up from the waiting chair and set the magazine he was reading down on the table. "Are you ready?" he asked.

I nodded then followed Brock out to his black SUV. Neither of us said a word as we got settled. Dr. Robison's words rang in my mind. *Men can't read your mind.* "Are we still friends?"

Brock squeezed his hands around the steering wheel so tightly that his knuckles were white. I didn't think he would answer me at first. I thought that would be it and he would tell me when we got to

Neal's that he planned to fire me. "I don't even know why you would ask if we're still friends, Daisy. You're like my sister. Do you know what I felt when I walked onto the dungeon floor to see someone in my club with you on that cross and blood running down your back?" He tightened his jaw. "Your actions upset me last night. I wanted to take care of you and kill the bastard. How could you even ask if we are still friends?" He glared at me.

I thought about my words. I needed to change my life. "You didn't talk to me last night or today. I thought you would fire me. Today in therapy, I realized why I did what I did, but I need to have that conversation with Neal and Aaron first."

"Daisy, you're not talking in third person."

"Dr. Robison and Dai—I spoke about it today. I want to change."

"I'm proud of you for trying to better yourself. Last night, I was mad at you for the scene at Club Sanctorum. If I had spoken to you then, I might've yelled or said something I didn't mean. I knew about your appointment today and that you needed to talk something out. I'm glad you figured out why you scened."

Brock slowly relaxed in the driver's seat. The traffic in Ft. Lauderdale at six o'clock normally didn't move, but we were about to make record time to Neal's penthouse.

Brock stopped at a red light and turned toward me. "I will always be here for you."

He guided the car to a stop in front of Neal's building.

"Are you going to stay down here? I don't think Neal wants me anymore after what I did."

Brock rolled his eyes and pulled me into a hug. "Neal still wants you. Don't get me wrong, he's mad, and when you heal, your ass will be red for a while. But that man cares about you. Now, go up and grovel."

I still wasn't sure that Neal loved me. I exited the SUV, waved goodbye to Brock, and hoped the conversation Neal and I were about to have would go as easily as it had with Brock. After I talked to Neal, I needed to call and talk to Aaron. The conversation would have been easier if Aaron and Neal were both in Ft. Lauderdale.

2

NEAL

"Did you talk to Brock again?" Aaron asked as he rubbed his eyes. I'd called him the second I hung up with Brock and explained everything that happened last night at the club. He jumped on a flight from California to Ft. Lauderdale after his dinner meeting.

Aaron sat on one of the kitchen stools at the counter and sipped a beer. I salted the water before I dropped in some pasta.

I didn't understand why Daisy scened the night before. Earlier, when we talked on the phone, she seemed fine. She hadn't asked another dom for a scene in six months.

The day before, I was in DC with President

Tucker. We were discussing new cybersecurity software when Brock sent me a text asking if I'd okayed Daisy to do a scene. I'd felt a mixture of betrayal and anger and had stormed out of the meeting to call Brock.

Aaron sipped his beer again. "I only talked with Brock once. Did you call him?"

"I talked with him last night after Daisy went to bed. I can't believe she let a scene go that far. We need to explain that she is only going to scene with us from now on."

Aaron nodded.

"Brock told me he banned the guy from the club. I'd never heard of him or seen him before."

Aaron had asked if I could wait to speak to her until he made it back. It took everything in me to stay in the penthouse and not drive to Brock's and demand answers.

"I have no clue what triggered her to do this." *Maybe it's time to let Aaron be with Daisy.* "Maybe you should take her to California."

Aaron sat his beer down and glowered at me. "Don't start that shit. She needs both of us, and you know it. Hell, I think you and I need each other, so stop. This relationship is a team, and we will fight for her together. Something set her off. Also, I still want to know more about this guy who drew blood from our sub. You have an evil grin. What did you do?"

"I took care of him. His name is Fredrick Carson. We shouldn't have anything to worry about again."

Aaron motioned for me to continue.

I stirred the pasta. "I couldn't sleep last night, so I looked into him before I did anything. He abused his ex-wife for years, and when she tried to leave him, he put her in the hospital and took full custody of their kid. Fredrick made up a bullshit story about how she was an unfit mother, but he doesn't even spend time with the kid. Fredrick did it for payback because she wanted to leave him. So I might've taken a video of the idiot beating his ex-wife off his phone and sent it to her. I also felt she needed money, so I drained one of his offshore accounts into hers. She should have enough money to fight the case now."

"God, I'm glad you're on my side. Thank you for taking care of him. On another note, Christmas is next week. Have you thought about what we should get Daisy? I think I'll wait until Christmas to tell her I'm moving in with you guys."

Last week, Aaron called and asked how I felt about him moving in with us. I had wanted it for a while, and I felt it was something Daisy needed. The only problem was that I had feelings for Aaron that he didn't know about. With him living here, I knew it would be harder to fake how I felt. If we wanted to make it work with Daisy, I needed to bury my feelings for Aaron. I drained the water off the pasta. "I thought you could propose."

Aaron rolled his eyes. "You need to stop putting yourself on the outside of our relationship. I wanted *us* to ask her to marry *us*."

Growing up, I was a burden to my mother. Over the years, I tried to position myself so no one would hurt me. Aaron was right—I needed to be a part of the relationship instead of hovering on the outside, waiting for it to fail. The penthouse had started to seem more like a home since Daisy moved in almost a year before. She slowly worked to add color to the bachelor pad, and I knew Aaron didn't think he could stay here if she wasn't with him. A vase of pink daisies sat on the counter. Each week, he had new daisies delivered because he knew how much she enjoyed them.

I grabbed my phone off the counter and sent Daisy a text telling her that Brock would pick her up.

I grated the cheese as a distraction before

answering Aaron. "It's hard for me to think that either of you would want to keep me." I didn't look up from the cheese as I spoke. "I feel like a timer is ticking on our relationship. I don't know what I would do if I lost either of you." It was the deepest feeling I had expressed to anyone in a very long time.

Aaron folded his arms across his chest. "I've never felt more complete than when I'm with you and Daisy. We need to build a bond between the three of us. I think you and I have sidestepped our feelings, as well."

My mouth went dry at Aaron's words. I thought I had hidden my feelings for him well. I didn't want him to leave Daisy and me. If he ever knew I had feelings for him... I dropped the cheese and grabbed a beer out of the fridge, which gave me time to think about how to respond without wrecking everything around us. I chugged half the beer, and it felt good. "I won't overstep my bounds, Aaron. I know where I stand."

Aaron cocked his head to the side before he stood and walked toward me. Finally, he was so close that I could feel his body heat. After his shower, Aaron had come into the kitchen without a shirt, and his sweatpants hung low. The moment I saw him, I decided to cook dinner as a distraction. "And where might that be?" he asked.

I wanted to reach out and run my hands down his body. In all my years, I had never let another man or woman top me. But something about Aaron drew my submission. "We each have a relationship with Daisy."

"Why can't you and I be in a relationship?"

My mind had a hard time with the words Aaron spoke. He was so close that my body leaned into him. "Because you like women."

Aaron reached forward, ran his hands through my hair, and pulled me in. His lips crushed against mine. He dominated the kiss, and my body was on fire. I felt his tongue demand entrance, and my body turned into putty under his touch. I was so lost in the kiss that I didn't hear the door open. Aaron pulled back, and a second later, I heard Daisy's heels on the tile floor.

He stepped back. "We're not done, but we need to talk to Daisy first."

Aaron had returned to the stool by the time Daisy walked around the corner. I peeled my eyes from the man who kissed me senseless and looked at the woman who held my heart. Her eyes were black with smeared makeup. She looked like she didn't think she was welcome.

Aaron

I had waited months to show Neal how I felt. I liked to have my hands on him. I wanted to dominate him. I hadn't only wanted Daisy the day I saw her in my parents' backyard. I remembered the second my eyes landed on her. She was an up-and-coming makeup artist to the Hollywood elite. One day, she disappeared, and I hadn't seen her for fifteen years until that day I came to my parents' house.

Over the years, I had seen Neal at Club Sanctorum. I had kept my feelings for him under wraps because of the Hollywood stigma against queer men, but I no longer cared by the time they were both in my parents' backyard—I had feelings for both of them. It took three months for me to worm my way into their hearts. I wouldn't let what I'd dreamed of for years fall apart. We needed to figure out what had upset Daisy then explain how the relationship would change. I knew she would be open to Neal and me. Daisy and I needed to figure out how to prove to Neal that he would always be a part of our lives.

I followed Neal's eyes to the woman who held my heart. When Neal called me in California, I felt helpless. It made the decision to move to Ft. Lauderdale so much easier.

Daisy stood there in her black yoga pants and white blouse. Her presence lit up the room. She had her dark hair piled on her head, and her gray eyes didn't have the sparkle they normally held. Neal walked over and wrapped her in his arms. She broke down, crying. I gave them a second before I walked over and pulled them both into my arms.

"Daisy's sorry," she sobbed.

"Let's eat first. Then we can talk about last night." One thing I knew I would change when I moved in was to make sure Daisy ate enough. The way she picked at her food had me wondering if her captor used to make comments about her weight. Every so often, I would catch her skipping something she wanted.

Neal and I led her to the kitchen bar, and Neal plated our food. I loved having the three of us together for dinner. It felt like family.

"Daisy wants to talk about last night."

"I want your full attention when we talk about

last night, and we'll get to why you scened with Fredrick. But he isn't the only point we need to talk about." I gave Neal a pointed look. "First, tell me your favorite part of Christmas."

Daisy's hand froze in midair. I could see her body tensed. "I don't like Christmas."

I glanced in Neal's direction, and he shrugged. It seemed he didn't know she didn't like Christmas.

"Okay, I'm up for the challenge of changing your mind. How about you, Neal? What is your favorite part of Christmas?"

Neal looked as caught in the headlights as Daisy had been by my question. It seemed as though I would have to work to change their thoughts about the magical time of year.

"Christmas was the only time of the year my mother would sober up. She did it so she could get me a gift."

Over the past three months, Neal didn't discuss his life growing up, but he said it had been hard. Daisy reached out, grabbed Neal's hand, and squeezed it. I wanted to grab his other hand and comfort him, but we needed to talk to Daisy first. Everyone around the counter ate in silence, all lost in their own world.

I looked over and saw that Daisy had finished her

food. I motioned to the living room. While Neal and Daisy got situated, I grabbed her a glass of white wine and beer for Neal and me.

Neal and Daisy curled up in the middle of the couch. I squeezed into the opening next to Daisy. I took my seat and rested my arm around the back of the couch so I could also lie my hand against Neal's shoulder. He looked over Daisy's head in surprise.

"Okay, Daisy, do you want to tell us what happened last night?" I asked, running my hand through the back of Neal's hair.

Daisy pulled her knees into her chest and exhaled. "When you mentioned we were going to California, Dai—I panicked, and I went back in time and wanted to erase the memories. The easiest way to clear my mind is subspace. I found the first free dom and inquired about a scene. Dai—I'm sorry. I know you guys don't want to be with me. Is it possible for you or Neal to be in a ménage? Both of you have public careers. I want to escape before I lose everything."

Holy shit. "Daisy, you just talked in first person."

Neal had a smile on his face.

"I talked to Dr. Robison today. She told me to think about what I said before I spoke. She said I use the third person to escape reality. Dai—I'm trying, it might take a while."

"I'm proud of you for trying to improve yourself. Now, let's talk about California. I wanted you both to go to my movie premiere. I don't care if Hollywood knows I'm in a ménage." When she went to speak, I put my fingers to her lips. "I planned to tell you on Christmas, but I think you need to hear this sooner. I asked Neal last week if I could move in with the two of you. I'm moving back here."

"Really?"

"You have the most beautiful smile, Daisy," Neal said, and then he looked at me. "Yes, he is moving in with us. Now tell me why the mention of California sent you into a spiral. We've talked about going to California before, and that didn't happen."

Daisy took a sip of her wine. "Talking about it and having an actual plan are two different things. Daisy hasn't been back since Sam carried me out of the evil man's house. Damn it. I meant *I* haven't been back."

"Daisy, it will take time. Don't beat yourself up about flipping back and forth. Take your time and work through it."

Neal and I were stupid for not thinking about how even mentioning California would affect her.

Daisy never talked about her years being held by a psychopath—but we also never asked her to. "Do you want to talk about your time while Al had you? If it's too hard, we don't need to go there. As for California, I want the world to know I love you and Neal."

"No, you have to go. I panicked, and I feel like you and Neal will get sick of me. I love you both so much." She started to cry.

"We love you too. I don't need to decide about California tonight. Let's talk it over for the next few days and decide. I need to make one thing clear. If something upsets you, come to Neal or me. From this point forward, you, Neal, and I are in a committed relationship."

"Okay," Daisy squeaked.

"Now tell us about what happened."

Over the next hour, Daisy talked about the things Al Scott, the low-life Hollywood executive, did to her. At one point, I decided that if Sam hadn't killed the fucker five years before, I would have killed him myself. But Daisy was strong and told us about her time even though it tore her apart to talk about.

"I'm glad you told us your story, Daisy. This is something we should've talked about months ago.

From this moment forward, we talk about anything that is bothering us."

Neal leaned forward. "I don't care if either of you thinks your issue is small. I want to hear it."

"Same for me. Neal and I have something to ask you. How do you feel about Neal and me also being together? We both love you more than our next breath, but Neal and I like each other. Are you okay with that?"

3

DAISY

Two days had passed since Aaron told me he and Neal had feelings for each other. After his declaration, the tension in the room evaporated, and the three of us got along better than we ever had. Excitement coursed through me. I couldn't wait to watch the two men I loved be together. I took a swig of my cold water, but it did nothing to cool my body.

"Daisy."

I jumped at the sound of Jessica's voice. "You scared the crap out of me. Are you working upstairs today?" Jessica, who worked for Alex Ross, Aaron's older brother, at Ross Enterprises, worked from Brock's office most of the time but worked remotely a couple of days a week. I glanced at her growing belly, and a twinge of sadness came over me. But Dr.

Robison said I shouldn't worry until I met with a doctor.

"I have a doctor's appointment today. Brock planned to go to the doctor with me, but something went wrong with his current mission. I haven't talked to you since the other night. Do you want to go with me?"

"Sure. Just let me tell Brock." I reached for my desk phone.

"I already told him I planned to ask you. Let's head out."

I locked my computer and sent Neal and Aaron a quick note telling them I was going with Jessica to her appointment then lunch. Sometimes, Neal stopped by with lunch, and I didn't want him to show up and worry why I wasn't at work.

I followed Jessica outside to her SUV. She barely waited for me to click the seatbelt before she fired off her first question. "Are you and the men okay?"

"Things at home are better. They're scared to touch me because of my back. But it looked good this morning. Dai—I was dumb to do what I did. I'm happy they forgave me."

"I can't believe how well you're doing with talking in first person. But I still want to know why you scened with Fredrick." Jessica grabbed my hand

and squeezed. "I understand if it's too private and you don't want to tell me. But I care about you and want you to know I'm here for you."

"Neal asked me to go to California for Aaron's premiere, and I panicked. Everything hit me at once. What will I do when they leave me? What will I do if I'm kidnapped again? The nightmares have finally slowed down, and now I'm going back to where it started. I would love to see my friends again in California, but I'm worried I'll panic when we touch the ground there."

"First of all, Neal and Aaron won't leave you. When Brock called Neal about the scene, he panicked. Brock had never heard Neal so worried. He left his meeting with the president of the United States and came back to Ft. Lauderdale, but Aaron wanted him to wait to talk to you. He spent the night destroying the life of the man you scened with."

"What do you mean he destroyed Fredrick's life?"

"Brock got his name then researched him. Fredrick is a bastard. He beat his wife. When she tried to leave with their kid, he divorced her and somehow got sole custody. Brock told me Neal found video evidence of him beating his wife and sent it to her along with money out of one of Fredrick's offshore accounts. Now, she will be able to fight him fair and get her kid back."

I couldn't hold back a smile. Neal used his hacking skills to help people. What he did probably wasn't within the law, but if he helped that woman get her kid back, I would be happy.

"He said nothing."

"When Neal and Aaron didn't call that night and Neal asked me to stay at your house, I figured our relationship was over. When I showed up to the penthouse the next day and Aaron sat perched at the counter, I didn't know what would happen."

Jessica shifted the car into Park, and I looked at the glass windows wrapping around the building. The clinic she went to was a state-of-the-art facility. I knew it was the clinic Brock used for his employees—he donated tons of money to make sure they had the latest and greatest of everything. It was no shock Jessica's doctor was there. "I think they needed time to cool down," she said. "They found out their girlfriend scened with someone without permission, which hurt both of their feelings."

When Aaron had mentioned that he was moving in with Neal and me, excitement coursed through my body. I loved Neal, but it felt like something was missing when Aaron wasn't around. "I think you're right. Aaron's moving in with Neal and me at the start of the year. I need to figure out my emotions so I can go to Aaron's premiere. I'm scared."

"Do you want Brock and me to come too?" Jessica asked, rubbing her belly.

I needed to face my past with Neal and Aaron, and I couldn't keep using the crutches I'd come to depend on. "No, but thank you for the offer. Let's get you checked in."

The scent of roses hit me when I opened the glass door. White rose bouquets sat on the entry table on the way to the check-in desk. No patients waited in the waiting room. As Jessica checked in, I took a seat in one of the leather chairs and grabbed the latest *Star* magazine on the table. Annabella's picture graced the front. Guilt hit me as I looked at her photo. Over the years, she'd tried to contact me, but I ignored the calls. I didn't blame her for what happened. I just didn't like to talk about my ten years of captivity.

It looked as though Annabella had set a date for her wedding. The nurse escorted Jessica through the hallway door, and I walked up to the receptionist. "Daisy—sorry—I was wondering if I could make an appointment with a fertility doctor." The young woman scrolled through her computer.

"We have a cancellation with Dr. Jones, she is normally booked months in advance and hard to get an appointment with. But her twelve o'clock appointment canceled. The appointment is yours if you want it, but I will need your medical card and license."

My hands shook as I dug in my purse. I hadn't planned on an immediate appointment. I was going to schedule something for next week then work up the courage.

The young girl behind the desk grabbed my hand as I put my medical card on the counter. "You have nothing to worry about. Dr. Jones is the best." Her soft voice calmed my nerves. I paid the copay and took my seat in the leather chair. I picked up the magazine to read Annabella's story, but the words blurred together. I didn't even hear Jessica walk up to my chair.

"Daisy, I'm so sorry, but Alex fired the HR manager at work. I need to get back to Ross Enterprises before Alex fires anyone else. Do you want me to call Mia to come get you?" Mia was one of Brock's mercenaries.

"No, the nice lady scheduled an appointment for me today. I'll text Neal and take an Uber back. But let's have lunch tomorrow."

Jessica gave me a quick hug before she ran out the door to fix her boss's issues. Alex couldn't hold his temper most of the time, but his bark was louder than his bite. They would eventually hire everyone Alex fired back at a higher salary.

"Dakota Michaels?"

I almost missed my name. It had been years since someone said my real name out loud.

A nurse in her late forties with light-brown hair waited for me at the door, holding a clipboard. Butterflies flew around my stomach.

She led me down the hallway and into a room then motioned for me to take a seat on the table so she could take my vitals. It felt as if my heart was about to beat out of my chest.

When she took me into the doctor's office, my hands were sweating and shaking. Dr. Jones's office was large. She sat behind a large glass desk, and baby photos lined the wall behind her. It made the room feel inviting.

"Hello, Dakota, my name is Dr. Jones. Please have a seat."

"Daisy likes—sorry," I mumbled. "Please call me Daisy." Like the woman up front, she didn't flinch at my words. She nodded, and I took a seat.

"Daisy, can you tell me a little about yourself and why you're seeking a fertility doctor?"

I couldn't help but twist my hands in front of me. It was hard to discuss my past. "Fifteen years ago, a sadist kidnapped me and held me captive. I was under his command for ten years. The evil man told me he made it so I can't have kids. I found two wonderful men, and I want to know if I can start a family with them."

I had to give credit to the doctor for not dropping her jaw. Most people thought my story was a lie until they discovered my back. It wasn't, and I had the scars on my body to prove the years of abuse.

"When was the last time you saw a doctor?"

"When Sam and his team rescued me, I saw a doctor, but my mind was a fog back then, and Daisy doesn't remember what they said."

"Have you had unprotected intercourse recently?"

"Yes, I belong to a BDSM club, and they do a yearly blood draw. I don't have an STD."

The doctor coughed to cover up a laugh. "I'm glad you don't have an STD." She grabbed her stethoscope and walked toward the exam table. "Let's do an ultrasound."

I followed the nice doctor over to the exam table and jumped up. The paper crinkled under my butt.

"Can I lift the back of your shirt and listen to your lungs?"

I nodded before thinking about it, and her breath hitched when she lifted my shirt. "I hope the man who did this to your back is in jail."

"Neal, one of my men, took care of him. He won't be happy for a while. Aaron, my other man, wasn't happy either."

"Your lungs sound good. Let's have you lie back so I can take a look at your reproductive organs."

The gel felt cold as she squirted it on my stomach. She pressed a device to my stomach, and the screen lit up. A thumping noise came through the machine. I glanced to the doctor, and Dr. Jones fixated her eyes on the screen. "Do you see what the problem is?" My voice shook.

"Well, Daisy, the reason you never got pregnant in the past is that you have an IUD. But I think your IUD is past its expiration—look here." She pointed to a speck on the screen. "It's one of your babies, and if you look here"—she pointed to another speck—"it's your other baby. Given their sizes, you're about four weeks pregnant."

I thought my ears were playing tricks on me. "Are you sure I'm pregnant?"

"Yes, and with twins." She wiped the gel off my stomach and handed me a picture with my two babies. "I can refer you to another doctor for delivery. We need to get this IUD out."

It took her a few minutes, and Dr. Jones removed the T-shaped device.

"Here is a list of doctors I recommend," she said when she was done.

"But I don't feel pregnant."

"Some women don't experience morning sickness. But, Daisy, you are pregnant—and with twins. You need to go home and tell your Neal and Aaron the excellent news."

When I stepped into the waiting room, Neal and Aaron sat together. "What are you guys doing here?" I looked toward the receptionist.

"She said nothing," Neal said. "When you texted you would be seeing a doctor, we wanted to be here to make sure you were okay."

I turned back to the receptionist and asked if I could schedule an appointment with Dr. Angel, and her face lit up. Dr. Angel was Dr. Jones's top OB-GYN on the list.

I turned to Neal and Aaron. "Do you guys want to come with me Friday to the next appointment?"

"Yes, but tell us what's wrong." Neal stepped forward and wrapped me in a hug.

"Nothing is wrong. We'll talk about it when we get home."

I finished confirming the appointment with the receptionist, and Aaron went to get the car. When he drove around to the front door of the clinic, I almost lost it. Aaron and Neal had a Christmas tree tied to the top of the Land Rover—it was so big that it hung off both the back and front of the vehicle. I had no clue how Aaron could see through the front window.

"Umm… Neal, do you think the tree is big enough?"

"Don't get me started. Aaron wanted three trees. I don't even know where he planned to put them. I talked him down to one."

I couldn't hold back my giggles. "Let's go home. I need to talk to you and Aaron." I reached into my pocket and texted Brock to let him know I wouldn't be back. If he needed me, he would send me a text.

Fredrick

I leaned back into my car and watched as the dumb bitch walked out of the clinic. She thought she could escape me. But she had another thing coming. Daisy would be mine again, and once I had her again, nobody would take her away.

My phone rang in the passenger seat and made me take my eyes off the target, the woman who would be under me again. She would be mine, and I looked forward to hearing the screams come out of her mouth once more. It had been so beautiful to watch the blood run down her skin.

"What?" I screamed into the phone.

"Sir, I have your one o'clock meeting here. Will you make it back? It's Judge Houser."

"Yes, I'm on my way."

After my meeting to get another issue handled, I knew I would get rid of her men and make her mine. I had the perfect place planned to hold her.

4

DAISY

The trip back to the house went quickly. I'd told the men we would talk when we got home, but inside my stomach turned—I didn't know if either of them wanted kids. I knew Neal had grown up in a difficult home, and I worried about him the most.

I noticed Aaron's phone wouldn't stop ringing. "Are you going to answer that?"

"Nope."

"Who is it?"

"My agent."

"You need to get that. What happens if he has a part for you?"

"He doesn't."

I looked in Neal's direction.

"Aaron told his agent today he plans to retire and move back to Ft. Lauderdale. Aaron's agent is mad that his cash cow quit."

Aaron grunted in his seat as he parked in the penthouse parking space.

"Are you sure you want to quit?" I got out of the car.

He jumped out of the car quickly then held me in his arms. "I want to be with you and Neal. I don't want Neal to have to move Black Hat to California, and you have too many bad memories there. I might work for my brothers, Alex and Antonio—they've offered. Hell, I've got so much money that I might open a charity or something."

"Okay."

He captured my lips and demanded entrance, and all my worries melted away as Aaron held me in his arms. I forgot where we were until Neal came up behind me and kissed the side of my neck. I needed to tell them what the doctor said, and we were still in the middle of a parking garage.

I panted. "We need to go inside."

A beautiful smile spread across Aaron's face.

I pulled back and rested my hands on my hips. "How are we going to get the tree to the penthouse?" I asked my men.

"Already taken care of," Neal said. "Frank, the building manager, will have a crew bring it up. You, my dear, need to tell us why you went to the doctor and why you made another appointment."

Aaron picked me up and threw me over his shoulder. "Let's get our woman upstairs."

Neal and I had moved into Patty's penthouse a few months before. She was Neal's boss and the owner of Black Hat. But last year when her father disappeared and her status as the next Queen was outed, she and Sam went to Shialia. She told Neal to move into her penthouse. She'd had all of her things moved into storage.

I couldn't help but stare at Aaron's ass as it flexed with each step. When I glanced at Neal, I caught him looking at the same thing, and we let out a laugh.

Neal opened the door for Aaron, and he carried me to the couch and sat me down on his lap. Neal sat right next to him, pulled my feet onto his lap, and rubbed them.

"Now, tell us what's wrong."

"I didn't tell you guys the whole story of why I didn't think you would want to be with me. It's not only my third-person talking I'm trying to fix, but the evil man told Dai—me—that I could never have kids.

He said, 'I never have to worry about you getting pregnant.'"

Aaron's arms tightened around me. Neal opened his mouth to speak, but I cut him off first. "Dr. Robison told me to see an OB-GYN before I jumped to conclusions. I haven't been on birth control for the past year, but nothing happened. Today, when Jessica went to the doctor, I asked if they had an appointment, and they had a cancellation."

"We would have gone with you. This isn't something either of us would want you to go through alone. We're a team." Neal always wanted to be by my side whenever I dealt with hardship. He told me one night that he wished he could sit with me through therapy because he didn't like how I got upset afterward and he wanted to know why. There were things I'd told Dr. Robison about my experiences that I still didn't feel comfortable telling my men. I knew that would change.

I squeezed Neal's hand. "I know. I didn't plan to see someone today. They said there was an opening, so I took it."

"What did she say?" Aaron's voice held concern.

I reached into my pocket and pulled out the sonogram. "We're having twins."

The words were barely out of my mouth when

Neal captured my lips. Aaron's hands went to my belly.

"This is the best Christmas gift ever," Aaron whispered in my ear.

"We're going to be dads," Neal whispered.

Aaron leaned back. "How did it happen? We've been having crazy sex for the past three months. Is there something we need to worry about?"

I gripped Aaron's hand. "No. He had a doctor put an IUD in me years ago. Dr. Jones thinks the IUD expired. She said I'm four weeks along. That was the last time all three of us spent time together. That means these buggers are part of all of us."

Aaron swung me in his arms and hurried down the hall. I looked over his back to see that Neal was a couple steps behind. He kicked open the master bedroom door and laid me down on the bed. Aaron's eyes held warmth and love, and I knew we would make it through anything.

"Aaron, are you sure she can have sex?" Neal grabbed my hand.

"Of course, I can have sex. Have either of you heard of a pregnant woman going nine months with no sex? You have to be crazy."

Aaron hadn't stopped peeling my yoga pants off my body. When his fingers brushed across my sex, I shuddered. "Neal, I believe Daisy needs us," Aaron said.

Neal's hand reached down next to Aaron's. He twined his fingers with Aaron's, and together they circled my clit.

"Hold still," Aaron ordered.

Neal broke away and climbed behind me, and I rested my back against his chest. He slowly worked his hands to the edge of my shirt then pulled it off.

"You have an erection," I said.

Both men chuckled. "We always have an erection when you are around." Neal skimmed his hand down the side of my body. "Your skin is like velvet," he whispered in my ear.

"I love you both."

"We love you too," Neal whispered as he unhooked my bra.

"I think our sub needs some swats. What do you think, Neal?"

"Why?" I asked.

Neal ran his hand over the scabs on my back. "For going to someone else when you needed us. For seeing a doctor about something we should've talked about. We need to communicate."

Aaron helped me move so I was lying across

Neal's lap. I felt his erection pulse as I wiggled in his lap, and Neal slapped my ass. "Hold still."

"Okay, Daisy, twenty swats. No count is required."

I felt the bed dip as Aaron kneeled between Neal's legs. Both men had removed their shirts, and their black slacks hung low. "Answer me."

"Yes, Si—"

Thwack. The sound echoed through the master bedroom. I welcomed the pain that spread across my ass. The bite of it went straight to my clit and released in jagged pleasure.

Aaron continued to rain the paddle down on my ass. Neal grabbed my hand and squeezed with each thwack that hit my ass. Aaron struck my ass fast and hard. The *thwack* of the hard paddle rang through the room every time it touched my soft flesh.

It didn't hurt. No doubt Aaron held back, merely letting me know he was in charge. My pussy throbbed with each strike, and he moved the paddle to the side before I orgasmed. I was close—only a couple more hits, and I would've gone over the edge.

He caressed my ass with his hand and slowly dragged his finger until he found my weeping pussy. "Neal, she is dripping wet. Her pussy is trying to suck my finger in."

"More."

Neal grabbed my chin, so I looked up at him. "More of what, love?"

"Anything. I'm so close."

I don't know whose hand it was, but one of my men brought a hand down five more times in quick succession, and I lost it. My body went over the cliff.

"Our little sub is so responsive."

Aaron

"I think I would like to see Neal go down on you while you wrap those pretty lips around my cock," I said.

Neal grunted his approval, and Daisy nodded and got on all fours. She had a brilliant smile I could get lost in when her pretty gray eyes looked up at me. Daisy ran her tongue over her lips. When she leaned forward and her pink tongue swept across my cock, I couldn't hold back the hiss, and the little temptress smiled. I needed to control her pace, or it would end too soon. I felt her moan across my cock, and when I looked behind her, Neal had his head buried in her velvety folds, and I could see his fingers pumping in and out of her.

Daisy continued to bob up and down, pulling my dick into her soft mouth. She reached out and cupped my sack, rolling it in her delicate fingers. I pumped my hips forward. My temptress sub continued to work my cock in her mouth, trying to speed up the pace. I tugged on her hair, and her gray eyes peered up at me.

"Bad girl. I don't want to come in your mouth, but you feel so fucking good. Flip around. I want to taste that delicious pussy."

She did as she was told, and I pulled her pussy to my lips and sucked on her clit. She rewarded me with a whimper, and Neal let out a groan. She had wrapped her pouty lips around Neal's cock and taken his big dick down her throat. The sight was amazing, and it made me want to pound into her velvety folds. I ran two fingers around her sex, and she bucked, trying to get penetration. I circled her clit another time before I slipped my fingers in.

Daisy pushed her hips back, trying to ride my fingers, and I slapped her ass. "Take what I give you."

I heard her whine around Neal's dick. When I looked at my other partner, I saw that his eyes were tightly closed. His fingers twined in Daisy's hair.

My fingers slipped in and out of her as I sucked her clit into my mouth, and she came apart on my hand. "I can't hold back any longer. Make Neal come in that pretty mouth."

"It won't be long," Neal grunted.

Daisy's legs spread for my pleasure. I couldn't wait to be inside her. Sex with Daisy was always amazing, but it wasn't sex. For the three of us, it was love.

"I love you, Daisy," I whispered.

She wrapped her hand around Neal's cock and looked back at me. "I love you too, Aaron. You two are my everything."

I ran my hands down her back, positioned my cock at her entrance, and slowly pushed it in. It was pure bliss. Daisy worked her mouth around Neal's cock at the same pace I moved in and out of her. When I started to speed up, Neal threw his head back and groaned. He was close, and I didn't know if I would last much longer.

Daisy's tight pussy felt so good. She pushed back against each of my thrusts. I wanted the three of us to go over at the same time, and based on the way Daisy's pussy clenched around my cock, she was close. I reached down and pinched her clit. "Now." The two most important people in my world went over the edge at the same time. I fell forward and pulled Daisy into my arms. Neal cuddled in next to us.

I had never been so happy. My phone rang in the living room, and I didn't want to break the spell of what we did.

"We need to get that."

"Nope. I want to stay in bed with you guys."

Daisy's phone rang next.

"Fuck, who could it be?" Neal grumbled.

I looked over at the clock, and somehow it was six o'clock at night. My nephew Ant's Christmas play was starting soon. Antonio, my older brother, had just gotten his son back, and he wanted his family at Ant's first Christmas play.

"It's my brother. Ant's Christmas play is tonight. I promised we would go. But I think he will understand."

Daisy jumped out of my hold. "We are not missing his play. I totally forgot. Let's go."

I pulled her back to me and captured her nipple in my mouth. Maybe I could get her to stay in bed.

She pulled back. "Let's go, or I'm holding out for a week." With that, she jumped out of bed, and Neal grumbled. Before we left the bed, I leaned over and kissed my man on the lips. He tasted like a mixture of the two people I loved.

5
―――
DAISY

I didn't know what to expect. I had never been to a children's play. The three of us hurried into the school gymnasium, where Antonio had saved us seats. Alex and Bridget held their two kids. Kat and Antonio both held up their phones to tape the stage, even though no one was up there yet. Aaron's parents sat in the front row with smiles on their faces. Sophie and Zane couldn't make it, as they were both in DC. Brock and Jessica rounded out the row of family and friends.

I took the seat between Neal and Aaron. The stage glittered with red, white, and green sparkles. When the lights dimmed, the Christmas tree lit up with an array of colors. Ten children pranced across the stage in a mixture of traditional Christmas costumes. Each kid searched for their parents and waved. When Ant's eyes hit our row, his face lit up, and his mom let out a whistle.

A petite blonde walked on stage and positioned the little children in their spots. Bridget had told me Ant was excited to be a shepherd. I had never been part of a school play. My stage fright had always been too bad.

I glanced around the auditorium, filled with parents and grandparents. A man in the back corner with his camera pointed at our row caught my attention. "Hey, Aaron, does it look like that guy is watching us and not the stage?" When we turned back around, the man had disappeared.

"I don't see anything, love."

I knew I didn't see things. I searched the crowd for him, but I couldn't find him anywhere. An uneasy feeling settled in my stomach.

Aaron gripped my hand, a reassuring smile on his lips. But instead of calming down, I felt my heart beat faster as I remembered that less than an hour ago, I was crying out in ecstasy as both he and Neal took me.

"What dirty thought just went through your head?" Neal asked in a hushed voice.

I elbowed him in the side. "You can't ask questions like that at a children's play. What happens if someone hears you?"

"You wound me, love." He laughed as he grabbed his side.

"The kids are on stage," Bridget said with a smile.

The teacher tapped the mic. "Thank you all for coming out for our annual Christmas show." She looked nervous, tightened her hand around the mic, and searched the crowd.

"This is my first year directing the Christmas pageant. So bear with me." The crowd let out a chuckle. I wanted to go up and hold her hand. "But over the past month of working with these little ones, they've stolen my heart, and I couldn't be prouder of the show they are about to put on. So if you can, put your hands together and welcome this year's talented students."

The teacher sat with her legs crossed, and the students' eyes locked on her as they sang their Christmas tune. I couldn't help but chuckle as a kid in the back screamed each word.

For the last song of the night, half of the students came forward to sing. Ant was front and center in his shepherd's outfit. I pulled out my phone to record my future nephew as he sang with his classmates.

When the song ended, Aaron pressed his hand to my belly. "Our kids will be up there soon."

I looked up and had to blink the tears out of my eyes. He was right—it would only be a few short years.

Neal put his hand over Aaron's. "I can't wait for our little girl to be the center of the stage. She's going to look just like her mom."

"How do you know we are having girls?"

Neal shrugged. "I don't, but I think we'll have one boy and one girl."

The petite blonde went back over to the microphone. "I would like to thank everyone who came out tonight. The show was better than I could ever have imaged. The students will be waiting in the back for their parents."

It was nice to know the school took security seriously. It would be easy to kidnap a student if they let them roam around a room filled with so many strangers.

Jessica wobbled over with her hand on her belly. "Is there something you need to tell me?"

"Let's talk after Christmas."

"Okay, but don't think I didn't watch you during the show."

I wanted to celebrate our news just with Aaron and Neal. I wasn't ready to let anyone else in.

Ant ran in my direction then wrapped his arms around my waist. "Did you see me sing, Auntie?"

I loved that he called me his aunt already. "Yes, I did." I leaned in and whispered in his ear, "You were the best singer and the best dressed."

"That's what Mommy said."

I looked up, and Kat had tears in her eyes. Every time the family got together, she seemed to tear up.

Neal pulled me into his arms. "Can we go? I so want your legs wrapped around me again."

Aaron came over "Ready to go? I want you both back in bed. I told Antonio you didn't feel well."

I rolled my eyes. "You two are insatiable. Take me home."

We spent the rest of the night making love.

Fredrick

The arrogant prick thought he could walk around after he destroyed my life. It wouldn't be long before I took everything that meant something to him.

It had been a close call when the whore spotted

me in the crowd. I knew she didn't realize who I was, but she kept looking for me after I moved. I had moved directly behind them. I wanted to reach out and kill the two men. It wouldn't be long before I destroyed them. I heard the conversation when they talked about Daisy being pregnant.

Too bad the bastards' fathers would never meet them. Because I would make her mine again, and she would pay for what she did.

6

DAISY

One morning, I overheard Neal and Aaron talking about meeting for lunch, and I wanted to surprise them and show up. My knee bounced under my desk as I waited for the clock to hit noon. The past couple of days had been amazing. Neal and Aaron couldn't stop talking about the twins. I had to stop Aaron from going on Amazon and ordering a whole nursery. I talked him into waiting for the new year.

The next day, I had an appointment with Dr. Angel to have a look at the babies, and then we were jumping on Aaron's jet and heading to California. My stomach churned at the thought of heading back there. I needed to face my fears, and I wanted to be with Aaron for his movie premiere.

Brock had a new client in his office, so I sent him a text to let him know I was heading to lunch.

When I exited out the back door of Blackwood Security to the employee parking lot, my phone chimed. A text from Brock flashed across the screen. He told me not to hurry back. I went to type a reply when I felt something push into my back, and a hand covered my mouth, muffling my scream.

"Walk toward your car, and don't even think about trying to escape. You and your boyfriends will pay for what you did." Fredrick's voice rattled my nerves. The moment he opened his mouth, I knew who he was. His stench was strong. I had a hard time holding back my vomit.

I climbed into my Acura MDX, which Neal had bought for me. He'd said it was the safest SUV on the road. When I turned to get a look at my kidnapper, I saw that his hair stood up from running his hands through it. Fredrick's white shirt had dirt caked to the front, and sweat streamed down the side of his face.

I noticed the gun he had pointed at my head. He climbed into the passenger seat and continued to point it in my direction.

"I'm sorry for what Neal did. I will fix it. Please let me go."

He didn't answer right away but instead ran a forearm over his forehead to wipe the sweat away. It almost looked as though he was coming down from a high and needed a fix. "Your boyfriend destroyed my life. He sent videos that tanked my career and started an investigation. The feds froze my bank accounts, and the money I had offshore is missing too. I know you guys took it."

I couldn't help but roll my eyes. Neal wouldn't have taken the money for himself. Jessica said he had given it to this crazy man's ex. I needed to figure out how to escape alive.

He shook the gun in my direction. "Drive."

I started the car and headed for the exit. "Which way?"

He gave me directions as we drove farther and farther away from the city. When he had me turn onto the part of I-75 also known as alligator alley, my stomach turned. The swamp was where people disposed of bodies. I needed to figure out a plan.

" We can work this out. Neal and Aaron will look for me." I wanted to get him to talk.

"Doesn't matter, bitch. You will be dead soon."

I clamped my hands on the steering wheel and watched as the swamp whizzed by us. The alligators were soaking up the Florida sun alongside the road.

"Why are you taking me out to the swamp, to kill me?"

"Your boyfriend owes me money."

"But if you kill me, he won't give you what you want. Let's head to the city, and I can call Neal."

His hands were shaking from the withdrawal. His stench filled the car and made it hard to breathe. I wanted to reach over to lower the window and gasp for air. If I didn't get fresh air soon, I might pass out or vomit in the car.

I touched my stomach and made a vow I would fight to save the three of us.

His phone rang, and he answered it. I could only hear his side of the conversation.

"Yes, I will have your money." He reached up and wiped off another layer of sweat. "I will have the money. Make sure you have my stuff. I will be there tonight."

The angry man clicked off the phone. "Make a right in half a mile."

"Please, let's go to an ATM, and I can pull out money."

"I want you to pay for what you did. You tricked me at the club. I want to watch the blood run down your skin as you beg for your life. Then I plan to send the recording to your men. It will be such sweet revenge if they have to watch you die."

Fredrick was crazy, and I didn't know how to rationalize with him. The road curved, and we passed a few side roads, which led to swamp houses. Those roads would take us farther into the alligator-infested area and far from help. I had to make my move soon, or he would kill me.

"Take the next turn, whore."

I slowly increased my speed as we got closer to the turn. He had his eyes trained on me and not the road. I cranked the wheel and took the corner at seventy miles an hour. The car tilted onto its side and rolled. When we had entered the car, I had put my seat belt on, but Fredrick's body flew from the car as it flipped. I gripped the steering wheel, trying to hold myself in place as the car continued to turn.

Glass shards hit my body, and I could hear the car crunch around me. My head swung and hit the side of the car, and I kept my eyes closed. The car rolled one more time and didn't seem like it was about to stop. I reached up to keep myself from hitting the ceiling. The car flipped again, and debris came through the window and hit my arm with so much force that I felt the bone snap.

We came to a stop upside down in the water. I

knew I had to run. Fredrick wasn't the only thing I needed to worry about. Alligators called the swamps home, and I didn't want to be their afternoon snack.

I reached up and unlatched my seatbelt with my good arm, and I fell to the roof of the car. My arm throbbed with pain, but I needed to get out of the SUV, which was filling with water. The front windshield had shattered into pieces when the car took the first roll.

I slowly climbed out the window. The shards of glass on the ceiling dug into my hands as I pushed myself through. Sand squished between my fingers as I crawled out, and water was rushing by me. The water was two feet high, and my knees sank the moment I moved forward.

I searched for a road or some other path out of the water. It wasn't only the alligators that worried me—the swampland was also full of water moccasins, not to mention the other dangerous animals that roamed the water. Alligator alley wasn't just the place to drop dead bodies—it was also where everyone took their unwanted poisonous animals. I heard rustling to my left and saw my kidnapper crawling toward me. He pulled himself out the side of the car and limped a few more feet.

The need to escape was strong. I tried to run in

the water, but with each step, my feet sank into the swamp floor. I had lost my shoes on impact.

"Stop, whore."

Like hell. I pushed through the pain as the ground cut my feet, and my arm hurt like a bitch. I didn't stop moving until I heard a gunshot. I stopped for a second and turned. He lay across the front of the SUV with the revolver pointed in my direction. My only choice was to continue to run. I didn't plan to be someone's captive again.

Another shot rang through the swamp as I tried to hurry my steps and watch for alligators. I counted each bullet he fired, holding my breath each time. He had fired five bullets. The fucker still had one left. I pumped my good arm and ran—I could see the highway up ahead. I was ten feet away. I needed to get to the road. He fired the last bullet, and I felt it graze my broken arm. I kept working forward and fought through the pain that radiated throughout my body.

With the road within reach, I didn't pay attention to my steps, and I tripped. I heard a growl as I went down into the swamp. The sound came from a furious alligator. I flipped onto my back and crab-walked away as well as I could with one arm sinking into the murky water and the other one broken.

A six-foot alligator had his eyes trained on me. I held back a scream. He took another step toward me, and I scooted along the swamp floor as fast as I could. As he took another step, I leaned forward and tried to stand back up.

Finally, with my footing under me, I went to turn, but I was a second too late. The gator lunged forward, and I jumped back and fell on my ass. Fighting through the pain and panic, I stood again, and just as the alligator was about the lunge, rustling on his left side grabbed his attention. I looked and saw my kidnapper standing there with his gun trained on me. He must have reloaded.

His finger was on the trigger. I turned to run when I heard the gun go off and he screamed. I felt the bullet hit my arm. It pushed me forward, and I couldn't catch my balance before my head collided with a rock and everything went dark.

7
———
AARON

Neal's office at Black Hat security in downtown Ft. Lauderdale was impressive. I couldn't pull my eyes away from the uninterrupted view of the Atlantic Ocean. The water sparkled under the Florida sun. In the distance, I could see a cruise ship heading south. Neal's office would give my arrogant older brother, Alex, a run for his money.

I hadn't realized how much I'd missed Ft. Lauderdale until I spent time with Neal and Daisy. I'd spent all my time inside when I was in Hollywood—the paparazzi never left me alone, but in Florida, they didn't bother me. It was refreshing, and I'd known since wrapping my last movie I didn't want to act anymore.

When I won my last Academy Award, the press

took it to a new level. If I opened the door for someone, they would make it look like I was dating the person. A month after I started to see Daisy and Neal, the media plastered my face across the pap magazines, saying I was dating my costar. Daisy saw the pictures and assumed we were no longer together, and I never wanted to hurt her again, especially since I got the news that we were having twins. I was still shocked that the three of us were going to be parents. Neal and Daisy didn't know how badly I wanted it.

The click of Neal's phone drew my attention from the horizon to the handsome man behind the desk. Neal ran his hand across his face.

"How's Patty?" I asked.

Patty was the owner of Black Hat. Since she'd left Ft. Lauderdale eight months before, Neal had taken over every aspect of the company. I could tell it had taken a toll on him. He didn't want to fail, so he worked extra hard to bring in more contracts. Black Hat was currently at capacity. They couldn't take on anything else unless they hired more help.

"Patty and Sam are still looking for her father. Her three brothers are no help, and she wants me to take over Black Hat permanently."

I shifted, walked away from the massive

windows that lined the office, and sat on the white couch. It was obvious by Neal's tone that he didn't want to take over the business completely, but Neal would do whatever she wanted. Patty had moved away when her father disappeared, and she was next in line to run the country.

"How do you feel about running the show?" I patted the white sofa for Neal to join me. I didn't have to ask twice. He left his black leather chair and sat next to me. His cologne was intoxicating.

"If she had called last week, I would have been excited. But Daisy will need us, and I want to be there for every step of our children's lives even if the twins aren't mine."

An urge to flog Neal came over me. I hated when he doubted himself. I knew it stemmed from his childhood. But he needed to understand that we were a team, and we stuck together. "I'm only going to say this once. These children are the three of ours. It doesn't matter whose DNA they have. We love them all the same."

Neal's body sagged next to me. He seemed worried that if the kids didn't have his DNA, I would claim ownership over them.

"Neal, you need to talk about things and stop keeping them inside. And as for Black Hat, you could merge with White Hat. Bridget could help you run this place. She needs help, and you need help. Why don't you combine the two?"

"Patty and I will discuss it more in March when we fly to Shialia for the wedding."

"Have they set a date in stone, or will it change again next month?" Sam and Patty had pushed the date numerous times due to issues with finding her father.

"Honestly, I don't know."

"Why don't you talk to Bridget now? Don't wait until March."

"I'll call her tonight."

"Now we have that settled, it's time for your punishment."

It took everything in me to hold back my chuckle when Neal's eyes widened. Neal and I hadn't played together yet, but the moment I walked into his office, my dick had gone hard, and I wanted his lips wrapped around it.

"Um...why am I being punished, Aaron?"

"That's ten more." I felt him shiver under my touch. "I want you to go lean over your desk." When he didn't immediately move, I added, "That's ten more."

He scurried off the couch and walked toward his

desk, but he glanced at the door. I had planned to play the second I pulled into the parking lot, and I locked the door on my way in. "Don't worry about it. I'm the only person who gets to see my subs naked. Don't keep me waiting."

I couldn't hold back the groan when Neal dropped his black work pants. He wasn't wearing underwear, and his dick looked hard. He wanted to play as badly as I did. I walked over and ran my hand over his firm ass. Neal pushed back for more contact. "Take what I give you, sub."

On the corner of the desk, I saw a ruler. It would work for what I had planned. I reached for the ruler and heard Neal's breath hitch. "Why are you being punished?"

"I don't know, sir."

"It's Master. I'm your master."

"Yes, Master."

I ran the ruler over Neal's ass before I pulled back and hit his ass three times in quick succession. He groaned under my hand, and his dick twitched. I reached around and stroked him.

"Please, Master."

I stopped. "Not yet, Neal. You don't come unless I tell you. Every time you doubt yourself as being a true part of our threesome, I will punish you. Those kids are both of ours. Do you understand?"

I didn't give him time to respond before I lay five more swats across his ass. "Please, Master," he panted.

His ass turned a beautiful shade of red. My dick pulsed in my pants, wanting to be deep inside him. I brought the ruler down in ten quick successions and grabbed Neal's cock. Its tip glistened.

"Unbuckle my pants, sub."

He moved from the desk and kneeled in front of me. Seeing the strong man in front of me almost made my knees buckle. His hands shook as he tried to hurry and unlock my pants. Within seconds, he wrapped his warm mouth around my cock and took me down his throat. I couldn't believe how good it felt.

I ran my hands through his hair, and he worked my cock in and out of his mouth. He looked up with his blue eyes, and I was lost in the man in front of me. If I didn't get myself under control fast, I would come in his mouth, but I wanted to take my time.

When Neal moaned against my cock and took me deeper into his throat, I had to bite the inside of my cheek to keep from exploding. I grabbed his hair and pulled him up off his knees. The second my lips hit his, he opened his mouth, and our tongues tangled together. I couldn't wait any longer. I needed to be inside him. I turned him around and pushed him down on his desk.

"Lube?" It didn't matter how badly I wanted him. I would never hurt Neal.

"Top drawer."

I grabbed the tube and greased up my cock and two fingers, which I used to loosen him up so he could take me. He squeezed around me as I entered, and it was pure bliss. I had to stop, or I would lose it. Neal pressed backward, trying to get me to move.

When I had control again, I moved in and out of him. It was ecstasy. I reached around, grabbed his cock, and stroked him. "Come, Neal." At my words, he exploded in my hand. I pumped in and out of him a few more times then lost it.

I leaned down and rested against Neal. We were both panting when my phone started to ring. At the moment, I didn't care about the call. I pulled up my slacks and walked to the bathroom to grab a wet cloth. Neal started to stand. "Stay," I said. "Let me take care of you."

I let out an aggravated sigh when my phone rang again. Neal worked his pants up as I walked toward my phone. The second it stopped ringing, the caller called again. My agent had been calling nonstop, and it was time to take care of the problem.

When I reached for the phone, it wasn't Harry's name on the screen. It was a blocked number. My finger hovered over the answer button as I debated. Something deep down didn't seem right. I clicked the answer button, and a low deep voice came over the phone.

"Yes," I growled.

"Is this Aaron Ross?"

"Yes."

"Hi, Mr. Ross this is Detective Higgins with the Ft. Lauderdale police. Daisy's car rolled ten miles down Highway 41. The ambulance is en route to the hospital."

The world spun around me. While Neal and I made love, our other half was injured. I couldn't dwell on that just then. "Is she all right?"

The officer let out a sigh. "Her car took a beating, but it protected her. I think she broke her arm, and she might have a concussion."

"We're on our way."

I clicked the phone off and looked in Neal's direction. "We need to go. Daisy's been in an accident."

8

NEAL

The car ride to the hospital felt like an eternity. Aaron pulled up to the valet, but I didn't wait for the car to stop before my feet hit the ground. A young lady sat behind the desk at patient services.

"I'm looking for Daisy Michaels," I said tersely. I wanted to reach across the desk and rip the keyboard out of her hands. I didn't need to turn around to know Aaron stood next to me. When the receptionist caught sight of him, her fingers stopped typing. Any other time, I wouldn't have cared about someone being starstruck by Aaron. But I wanted to get to Daisy. "Did you find her?"

"We have nobody by that name." She seemed bored.

"I meant Dakota Michaels. Can you hurry up?"

Aaron gripped my shoulder. I knew he wanted to curb my attitude, but I didn't care if I hurt the young girl's feelings. I wanted to see Daisy.

"She is still with the doctors. A nurse will find you when they have an update."

Waiting to find out if she was okay was going to drive me crazy. I wanted to be by her side. I leaned forward to give the young lady a piece of my mind when Aaron grabbed my arm and pulled me to the side.

When I turned in his direction, he had his phone against his ear. He pressed his lips into a thin line as he answered questions on the other side.

"I want to know where Daisy is."

Aaron grabbed my hand and gave it a squeeze. At the same time, the front doors to the hospital swooshed open, and Antonio Senior and Martha Ross burst in. I tried to pull my hand away, but Aaron gripped it tighter and narrowed his eyes at me.

We had talked about the three of us being together in private, but I didn't know how he felt about his family knowing. When Martha's eyes landed on Aaron's hand holding mine, her eyes lit up, and she came and gave me a hug. "I'm so happy you guys are figuring this out. Now, we need for Daisy to be okay," she whispered in my ear.

"Where is my daughter-in-law?" Antonio demanded. His voice echoed through the lobby. Aaron still had the phone pressed to his ear, and the conversation looked heated. When he finally hit the end button, his mom pulled him to her in a hug. He dropped my hand and wrapped both of his arms around his mother.

Aaron gave his attention to his father. "According to the chief physician, all we can do is wait in the ER waiting room. Since she is not our wife, he won't tell us anything. According to her medical records, Brock is her medical contact." Aaron held up his hand to stop my impending outburst. "She probably never remembered to change it after Sam and Brock rescued her. I will have it changed by the end of the day today, and I don't want to wait much longer to make her our wife. I hate not knowing."

"This is ridiculous," Antonio said. "I've donated millions to this hospital, and I want to know how my future daughter-in-law is."

Aaron let out a sigh. "Dad, you can't use your donations as leverage. They were donations. Brock will be here in a few minutes. I'm going to see if Detective Higgins can meet us in the waiting room and tell us what happened."

I stretched my fingers, missing Aaron's warm touch. It helped ground me.

From the first moment I sat in the teal-green chair, I was transported to my childhood. The smell of the waiting room brought back memories I would just as soon forget. Between the ages of three and five, I spent a lot of my time in that exact waiting room. The only thing to change was an updated coffee pot, and the TV was a flat-screen. It seemed the hospital still had the same kids' table and toys in the corner. I used to spend hours at that table while my mom had chemo. Dad never came with us—he spent that time drinking and blaming my mom for her cancer.

I spent hours with the nurses. They even bought me a cake on my fifth birthday, and we celebrated another year with them. But it would turn out to be one of the worst days of my life.

Dr. Larson had walked in and asked the nurse to contact my father. His eyes had a sheen. He had been my mother's doctor for years, and he would come out and spend time with me sometimes. I asked if I could take a piece of cake back to my mom. I hadn't understood what had happened yet. Betty, a young nurse, wrapped me in a hug and told me she needed to call my dad. When my father wouldn't pick up the phone, Betty sat with me through her shift change. Three hours later, when he still didn't answer, she took me to the cafeteria for dinner. We sat waiting for my father for six hours, and when he showed up, she told him my mom died. My dad turned and walked out of the hospital. Betty ran after him and told him he forgot me. I will never forget his words. "I don't want to see him. He is the reason my wife died." My dad turned on his heels and walked out of the hospital.

The sound of a soft voice took me from the horrible memory. "Is that you, Neal?" a woman in her late sixties asked, holding her hand to her mouth, with tears in her eyes.

Aaron grabbed my hand, but I couldn't pull my eyes away from the woman in front of me. "Betty?"

"Oh my God, it is you." She wrapped her arms around me and pressed a kiss to my cheek. I heard Aaron grumbling next to me. I had to give her a one-armed hug because Aaron still had my hand in his.

"Betty, I would like you to meet my partner, Aaron."

Aaron reached out and shook her hand.

"Betty used to watch me while my mom had her chemo treatments."

Aaron's head whipped in my direction, and I

shook my head. It was a conversation I needed to have with Aaron and Daisy.

"It's nice to meet you, Aaron." Betty turned back in my direction. Her gray hair had fallen out of her bun. "What are you doing here?"

"They rushed our girlfriend and the mother of our children to the ER, and we're waiting on some news."

Betty didn't have time to ask any questions before Aaron's dad beamed. "I'm getting another grandchild?" he asked.

"I'll get an update and be right back," Betty said.

Aaron leaned over and whispered in my ear. "You need to tell us about your childhood." He squeezed my hand and turned in his father's direction. "Yes, Dad, you are getting another grandbaby. We wanted to wait for her appointment tomorrow before we said anything. We're supposed to fly out on Saturday for the premiere and then to Denver for Christmas. I plan to move in with Daisy and Neal."

I held my breath because I didn't know how they would take it.

But instead of thinking we were strange, Antonio Senior stuck out his hand. "Welcome to the family, son."

I had to blink back tears. So much was happening, and Daisy wasn't with us. Dread filled my stomach, and I wanted to scream.

Betty walked through the door with a smile. "It seems I have a lady demanding that someone let her men back with her. If you'll follow me, I will take you to her."

Aaron and I were both next to Betty in seconds.

"We'll let everyone know you went back," Martha told us as we walked through the doors.

Betty pulled back the tan curtain around Daisy's bed. Her right arm was in a pink cast, and her left arm, into which an IV ran, was bandaged. I rushed to her side and grabbed her hand. I leaned down and gave her a kiss on the lips. Aaron also leaned down and gave her a kiss.

"You came."

"Of course! I will always come for you. I don't want to go through not knowing again." Aaron leaned in closer. "I felt so helpless when they wouldn't give us an update."

I cut Aaron off. "How are you? How are the babies? What happened?" I had a million questions running through my head.

Daisy let her head fall back onto the pillow. "Daisy is fine. I mean, I'm fine. My new OB-GYN is here. Dr. Angel will be down shortly. The nurse said the babies looked healthy, but she wanted my doctor to double check."

"What happened, Daisy?" Aaron asked.

She bit her lip. "Um, the guy I scened with wasn't happy with me. He didn't like how I got him banned from the club."

"I'm going to kill him." I couldn't hold the words back. Killing him electronically wouldn't be enough for what he did to Daisy. He put the woman I love in the hospital, and I wanted him to die.

A man who'd entered the room as I spoke said, "You won't have to kill him. An alligator took care of him. Daisy's lucky a patrol officer saw an object in the swamp. Officer Jacona reached her in time—an alligator was headed her way." He turned to her. "Hi, Daisy, I'm Detective Higgins. I was wondering if you felt up to telling me what happened?"

"Can we come in tomorrow and give a report?" I wanted Daisy to rest.

"I'll talk now. I don't want to deal with the police station tomorrow."

Daisy spent the next half hour explaining what happened. My vision turned red by the end of her story. He was already dead, and I wanted to kill him again. Aaron pressed his lips together, and his jaw twitched with each word. When our eyes locked, I knew he wanted to kill the guy all over again too.

Detective Higgins wished Daisy well then exited the room.

For ten minutes, Aaron's phone had been going off like crazy in his pocket. I didn't know how he could ignore it. I wanted to reach over and answer the phone. "Aaron, you need to get that."

"No. I'm spending time with you. Whoever it is can wait."

"Take it now," Daisy said. "We're just waiting on the doctor and my discharge papers."

He reached for his phone, and when his eyes landed on the screen, he went pale. "That motherfucker," he mumbled.

"What's wrong?" I asked.

"I'm sorry, I wanted us to tell the world about our relationship. My ex-agent threatened me yesterday, saying that if I didn't take a new role, he would tell the world about us. I told him to go ahead. I didn't think he would do it. I'm sorry this happened. The media have pictures of us."

Daisy reached out and grabbed both of our hands. "At least they got my good side. I don't care what the media says as long as I have you two."

"I don't think we should—"

"Don't you say it, Aaron," she said. "We are going to California. This is your last premiere, and we aren't going to miss it just because the media wants a picture. I don't care what the media says about me. I want to go."

A young female doctor walked in just as he was opening his mouth to respond.

"Hi, Daisy, I know we have an appointment tomorrow. But given the accident, let's take a look at those babies."

Daisy's face lit up at the mention of our babies. It only took the doctor two minutes before our babies were on the monitor and I could hear the heartbeats of our twins.

When I looked at Aaron, he had tears in his eyes, and Daisy had a big smile across her face.

9
DAISY

Two days had passed since the accident. Even though Fredrick had died when an alligator ate him for lunch, Aaron and Neal wouldn't leave my side. Finally on my own, I reclined back into a massage chair. Aaron and Neal had booked a mani-pedi for me, followed by getting my hair and makeup done. The paparazzi had run with the story about Aaron. The three of us didn't care that the media had plastered our relationship across the TV. Our close friends already knew about us, and that was all we cared about.

Aaron wanted to be out of the public eye by the time the babies came. When the doctor performed the ultrasound, both men had tears in their eyes. I swear if I hadn't been in the hospital, Aaron would've gone to the closest baby store and bought everything he could find. Every so often over the past couple of days, I would find him on his phone, looking at baby stuff. I couldn't imagine how many boxes would be arriving at the penthouse over the next few weeks.

We planned to go look at a house next to Aaron's brothers the following week. He wanted our kids to grow up close to their cousins. Neal and I had no brothers or sisters, and Aaron's family had taken us in like we were their own. I had no issues with living next to them.

The doorbell over the spa door rang, and when I looked in that direction, I couldn't hold back the tears. Annabella stood at the front door. Aaron had mentioned he had a surprise for me at the salon, but I'd expected a gift, not my old friend and boss.

When she spotted me, she ran in my direction. After I returned from being kidnapped, I cut out everyone from my past. I couldn't face anyone and didn't want to talk about what happened. After the first year, everyone from my past stopped contacting me, and when I felt better, I didn't contact them.

"Daisy?"

I leaned over the side of the chair and engulfed her in a hug. "Yes."

She climbed into the maroon chair next to me. Everyone wanted Annabella in their next movie. Her long blond hair shimmered in the light, her emerald eyes were piercing, and her hourglass figure filled out her jeans and white T-shirt perfectly. She placed her Prada purse on the table and slipped off her Prada high heels. I wanted to reach over and cradle her shoes. They were to die for.

"Dais—I mean, I take it Aaron called you?"

She crossed her arms and let out a huff. "I would have preferred that you had called."

The technician took that moment to rub my feet. It helped reduce the tension. So much time had passed, and I wasn't sure what to say. "After everything, I didn't want to talk to anyone. Al held me captive for ten years before Sam and his team saved me. I felt dirty and unworthy—that's the only way I can explain how I felt. Dai—I didn't want to talk to anyone. Then when I felt better, it had been too long. You were an A-list movie star. Why would you want to associate with me?"

Annabella reached over and grabbed my hand. Hers was soft and warm. "Daisy, we were friends—no, we *are* friends, and friends stick by each other through thick and thin. You know I don't care about the A-list title the media gives me. It hurt that you never reached out to me and dodged my calls. You know how excited I was when Aaron called me? No kidnapping will ever change the way I look at you."

"Even though I avoided you for so many years and I'm dating two men?"

She let out a chuckle. "I love you for the kindhearted woman you are. You would sacrifice yourself for anyone. I wish I had tried harder to help find you." Annabella's emerald eyes lost their sparkle. "I blame no one but Al for your years in captivity." She shook her head. "Okay, let's stop talking about the past. Tell me about those two sexy men you captured."

"Before we get to them... I saw you're getting married."

She let out a sigh. "It's not what it looks like. We are marrying for convenience, and I don't want to talk about my fucked-up situation. Tell me about those men."

I made a mental note to dive into her issues more later. Annabella and I spent the next two hours talking about Aaron and Neal.

Neal

I would never get used to how salespeople treated Aaron when we walked into stores. Aaron and I had set Daisy up with a spa appointment so we could go ring shopping. Daisy thought we were heading back to Ft. Lauderdale on Monday, but Aaron I had planned to spend Christmas at his house in Denver. His family and our friends were flying in to go skiing and spend the day with us.

The salesperson literally had drool running from his mouth the second Aaron walked into Tiffany's. When we said we were looking for an engagement ring, he escorted us to the back room and laid out a bunch of huge diamond rings, but none of it was anything Daisy would want.

"Do you have anything smaller and pink?" I asked.

"Every woman wants a big diamond," the man countered.

Aaron leaned back in a white chair and gazed at the diamonds. I knew one thing about my partner, and that was he didn't like when someone didn't listen to Daisy or me. "I believe you misunderstood us. We want to see a smaller pink diamond, or we can go somewhere else."

The middle-aged man looked flustered. He

pulled at his necktie before getting up and leaving to find us what we were looking for.

"You know, I think we should also get her a diamond collar," Aaron said.

Aaron and I had talked for hours about who would marry Daisy. We decided I would marry her and he would have a collaring ceremony with her. We planned to do the ceremony when we got back to Ft. Lauderdale. Deep down, I wanted to wear Aaron's collar too, but I wasn't ready to talk about it. We had met with a lawyer earlier to bind Aaron and me together financially, so if anything happened to either of us, the kids and Daisy would be okay. All that was left was for us to make her our wife.

"Here," the shopkeeper said as he returned. "I hope this is more to your liking."

It was a perfect pink teardrop diamond on a white-gold ring. The pink diamond had two white diamonds on the sides. I knew she would love it.

"We'll take it," I said. "We also need two matching wedding rings for men."

Aaron and I looked at rings and picked out one we both liked, and then we found a beautiful diamond choker for Daisy. Aaron whipped out his black card when it was time to pay. I protested because the ring was supposed to be from Aaron and me.

"It's our money," he said. "Can you grab us a drink while I finish paying?"

I left the store excited for our next chapter. That night, we were going to the premiere of Aaron's movie, and in two days, we would be in Denver celebrating with our friends. I couldn't wait.

10

AARON

I loosened my tie as we walked into the after-party for my latest movie, hosted by the director of the film. Neal, Daisy, and I went to show face then leave. I couldn't wait to peel Daisy out of her red dress, and Neal looked hot as hell in his black tux. I had a hard time concentrating on the questions the press asked earlier—all I could think about was getting them home and naked.

Daisy was excited and nervous as we pulled up to Ryan Hemsworth's house. She couldn't wait to see some of her old friends. She hadn't stopped talking about her spa treatment with Annabella and how they planned to meet up in Ft. Lauderdale. I knew Daisy attended the party for me, and she had been on edge the whole time. She tried to hide it, but I could see how tense her shoulders were.

The premiere went off without a hitch, and everyone seemed to love the movie. On the red carpet, the press wanted to talk more about my relationship than the amazing movie, thanks to my ex-agent for broadcasting our relationship to the world. The paparazzi had taken it to a whole new level.

I brushed Daisy's blond curls from her shoulder. Her vanilla scent consumed me and made my dick hard. "Have I told you how stunning you look? I can't wait to get you out of this dress."

Her breath hitched, and a blush came over her cheeks.

When I stepped back, Neal had started a conversation with a new and upcoming app developer in Hollywood. It sounded as though he wanted to hire Neal to figure out extra security for his company. I never understood half the things Neal talked about, but when he talked about computers, his eyes lit up, and I enjoyed seeing him happy.

I couldn't help but stiffen when I saw the head of the studio heading in our direction. Hollywood wasn't taking me leaving well. Everyone felt like I owed them. I owed no one—I came out and made it on my own. These men milked the money I brought in. They needed to find their next big actor because it wasn't going to be me.

James Archer had to be in his late fifties, and even with all the money, he hadn't aged well. His stomach hung over his expensive Armani suit, and the buttons on the front looked close to popping. James's hairline had receded since the last time we spoke.

He reached out his hand. His handshake was limp and cold. "What is this I hear about you leaving the business?"

Daisy stopped talking to the couple beside us and tensed when she heard James talk. I was about to ask her something when she said she had to use the bathroom.

I turned to go with her when James put his arm on me. "I think your lady can go to the bathroom by herself, though she is a fine piece of ass. Someone might hit on her."

It took everything in me to not punch the fucker in his wrinkly face. "So help me God, I will work to ruin your life if you ever speak about my woman that way again."

He puffed his chest out. "Be happy you're out of Hollywood, because after that threat, I would make sure of it. From what people have told me, she wasn't that good anyway. I can't believe the great Aaron Ross picked up someone's used slave and a kid from the hood as his gay partner."

I reared back to hit him in the face. When someone caught my arm. I looked at who would dared stop me from killing the fucker.

"Aaron, he isn't worth hurting your hand over. I'll take care of it when we get back to Ft. Lauderdale." Neal winked before he let go of my arm. It looked as though the head of the studio would lose his job next week. If the man had ever done anything wrong, Neal would find out and make sure he got what was coming to him.

The party had stopped to watch what was happening. Ryan, the owner of the house and a top director at every studio, walked over. "I think it's time you leave, James. This is Aaron's party, and if you can't respect my guest, you're not welcome."

"You can't tell me to leave. I will ruin you."

Ryan let out a chuckle. "Try and do that. I will take my business to the other studios. You can't ruin me. That doesn't work anymore, you ignorant asshole."

"Funny," I said, "he threatened me with the same thing. I'm not even in the industry anymore. I think he's trying to hold on to what little power he has left before the studio kicks his ass to the curb."

I didn't want to deal with the overgrown baby anymore. I looked to see where Daisy had gone, so I didn't see it coming until the fucker swung at me, and I saw it a second too late, but Neal punched him square in the nose and knocked him to the floor. Blood oozed out of his nose, and he groaned.

"Neal, are you okay?"

"Yeah, he's not the first person I've punched out." Neal's eyes turned dark, and I wanted to ask another question but resisted. "Go find Daisy," he said. "I will take care of this."

Daisy was near the bathroom, and it looked as if she was shaking. Annabella stood with her. When I reached her, I pulled her into my arms. "What's wrong, love?"

Daisy

The moment I heard the man speak, I knew my past wouldn't stay hidden. I had made it twenty-four hours before I encountered one of the men who'd tortured me for hours. The second his squeaky voice spoke to Aaron, chills ran down my spine.

He was more evil than the man who kept me in a cage for years. I wanted nothing more than to take him out in that second. But I froze and didn't know what to do.

It was the first time I had ever seen his face. He always wore a mask, and I didn't know if I did something, whether it would hurt Aaron's career, or if Aaron and Neal would believe that the man who'd made me bleed and given me most of the scars on my back was in the same room with us.

Instead of confronting my past head-on, as Dr. Robison always told me to do, I ran. Annabella stopped me before I could make it to the bathroom. My stomach churned, and I didn't know if it was morning sickness or the evil bastard in the room. I had a feeling it was because of the man.

Aaron walked up while Annabella tried to get me to calm down. "Love, what happened?" he asked, glaring at Annabella.

"You put that glare away, Aaron Ross. I stopped her as she was about to run past me. When you walked up, I just got her to take a deep breath."

I hated that they spoke about me as if I wasn't in the room. Yes, Aaron had his hand in mine, but his gaze was on Neal and the man from my past.

I took a deep breath. "That man you were speaking to used to come to Al's house."

Aaron's eyes flashed with anger. "Annabella, stay with her. I will be right back."

I tried to reach for Aaron, but he was out of arm's reach in seconds. I yelled his name, but he didn't slow down. When I started walking in his direction, Annabella wrapped her arms around me. "He needs this, Daisy."

I needed him more. Neal had a hand on James when Aaron got there. I heard him call him a pathetic piece of shit before he punched him in the face and gut. Neal grabbed Aaron and pulled him back. I escaped Annabella's arms and ran toward my men. "Aaron, stop. Let's call the police, and they can take it from here."

The piece of shit wiped the blood from his mouth. "You little bitch. You think you can ruin me like you ruined Al? I won't go down for what you think you know."

Neal turned in my direction and scooped me into his arms. "I'm taking her to the other room," he said to Aaron. "I think we should call Brock. The case is still open. He isn't the only man Brock has been looking for."

We went to the kitchen with Annabella on our

heels. Right before we walked around the corner, I saw Aaron pull out his cell phone. I let out a sigh of relief that one more creep would be off the streets. The only thing I worried about was the other women he had tortured in the past five years. I knew there was no way he had stopped when Al got arrested. James thought he was bigger than the law.

Annabella handed me a glass of wine, and I had to decline even though it would have helped with my nerves. "I can't. I'm pregnant." I hadn't planned on telling anyone but our family until we were further along. But I knew Annabella would have pestered me until I took a drink.

She squealed with excitement. "Oh my God, that is so cool."

"Shh. We've only told family. I just knew you wouldn't stop trying to get me to drink."

Annabella's excitement notwithstanding, the party had died down, and I felt bad because we had only been there for a half hour before I wrecked it.

"Baby, I will make sure he goes to jail," Neal said.

"That's not why I'm upset. I wrecked Aaron's party. This was his last one."

Neal pulled me into his arms. "Aaron didn't want to come tonight, but he knew a bunch of your old friends would be here. He came to make you happy. The fucker in the living room wrecked the party. He started something with Aaron before we even knew what he had done in the past."

I lay my head on Neal's shoulder and took in his warmth, but soon, the sound of footsteps heading in our direction made me pull away. Aaron stood in the doorway, his hair mussed from running his hands through it. His tie was completely loose, and he looked sexier than ever.

"Let's go home. I need both of you now," I said.

"Do I need to make a statement?" Aaron asked.

"No, Brock is flying in. He will take care of everything."

Aaron wrapped his arms around Neal and me. "Let's get out of here."

11

AARON

I couldn't wait to get home and wash away the bad memories of the night. We were leaving California soon, and I never wanted to go back. How could people I'd worked with over the years be such heartless bastards? Adrenaline coursed through my body. Neal reached over and grabbed my hand. The party had proven how well Neal and I worked to protect each other and keep Daisy safe. There was no doubt in my mind that Neal would help me hide the body if I ever needed to. We would do anything for Daisy.

"When we get home"—I paused until I had Daisy's attention—"I want you both to go upstairs and get ready." I let out a breath. "I need to be close to both of you tonight."

I had never been so angry. Daisy's past—and her terror—coming to the forefront only twenty-four hours after she'd arrived in California had my nerves on end. I wanted her experience to be magical, not to bring back nightmares from her past. "I swear, if I see that man again, I'm going to beat the shit out of him. You won't be able to stop me next time. I'm sick of people in power thinking they can do whatever they want because they have money. I want to work to bring people like James down."

"You gave James a few good hits before I pulled you off. Who knew the pretty-boy actor could fight?" Neal asked.

"Anyone who threatens you or Daisy, I will punish. After what I saw tonight, I want to work more at the women's shelter to help other women." I pulled Daisy in to my side. "I'm sorry you had to see that bastard."

"It sucks I had to see him, but now he will get what he deserves," she replied.

I captured Daisy's lips before the limo came to a stop in front of the house. I could never get enough of her or Neal. Life might suck at times, but as long as we had each other, I was okay.

"Go upstairs. I'll be up shortly." I adjusted my pants. "I can't wait to fuck you both."

Neal mumbled something to Daisy before he swooped her into his arms and took her upstairs. My phone vibrated in my pocket. I looked at the screen to see Antonio's name.

"Antonio."

"Do you need me to head to California?" One thing I liked about Antonio was that he always got straight to the point.

I took a swig of the scotch I'd poured. "No, Brock will land in a few hours and work with the FBI. I told him to call you if he needs help."

Antonio cleared his throat. "How's Daisy?"

That was the million-dollar question. "I think she's stronger than we treat her."

"Okay, see you in a couple of days. And, Aaron?"

"Yeah?"

"You need anything, and I will be on the next plane."

We said our goodbyes. I had the two people I loved more than anything waiting for me upstairs. I took the steps two at a time, and I heard laughter coming from the master bedroom. I stopped in the hallway just to hear how happy they were. It washed away the dread from earlier in the evening.

I entered the room. "Neal," I said, "I think Daisy has too much covering her skin."

Neal walked behind Daisy and slowly unzipped her red dress.

"Daisy, you are the most stunning woman I've ever seen." The red dress pooled at her feet. "Why don't you give Neal a kiss for helping you with your dress?"

Neal and Daisy pressed their bodies together. Watching the two people I loved kiss turned me on even more. Pure, unadulterated lust welled inside me. "Daisy, how about you help Neal take off his shirt?"

Neal's eyes met mine. I could tell he was completely lost in the moment. Daisy slowly unbuttoned Neal's shirt. With each button, she leaned in and kissed his chest. She looked hot as fuck in her black lace bra and panties. But it was the six-inch high heels she kept on that made me groan.

When Daisy reached Neal's pants, she dropped to her knees and slowly worked at his zipper. She knew she was driving us crazy, and I didn't care. A decadent smile spread across her face before she wrapped her pouty lips around Neal's cock.

"Neal, I know you are enjoying Daisy's mouth wrapped around your cock, but I think our temptress needs some attention of her own." Neal reached down and pulled Daisy up. He captured her lips before he tossed her on the bed.

I couldn't help but watch Neal's ass flex as he crawled across the bed and pushed Daisy's knees apart. He shoved his face into her waiting pussy. Daisy moaned as Neal licked her pussy. I wanted a taste but could wait for Neal to get her off. It turned me on to watch them be together.

"Spread your legs more, love," Neal mumbled.

I walked over to the chest in the bedroom and grabbed a bottle of lubricant. Our dear Daisy wouldn't need lube, but Neal would. I squirted lube on my hand and continued to watch as Neal licked her. It would be the first time Daisy saw me make love to Neal. We had talked about it over the past few days, and each time she was aroused and wanted us to be together. I shifted my painfully hard erection.

Tonight, they would completely be together. It was the beginning of our future.

"Daisy, I want you to move up," I told Daisy as I removed my pants. "Neal, I want you to enter our woman and then stop."

Neal quickly pressed his hard cock into her, groaning as he pushed in. I could see Daisy tilt her hips to take more of Neal's member. Instead of stopping, Neal worked his cock in and out of her. She threw her head back on the pillow and let out a groan.

I could never get enough of those two together. I enjoyed the show they were putting on.

Neal looked over his shoulder and locked eyes with me. "Join us."

"Does her pussy feel good?" I asked as I wrapped my hand around my cock.

"Fuck, yes." Neal pushed into Daisy and stopped. "She's so tight. Come and join us."

My cock twitched at the thought. I couldn't wait to be in Neal again. I ran my hand up Neal's back, pushing him into Daisy. I could no longer hold back. I tapped his leg. He never stopped thrusting into Daisy as he spread his legs. I groaned at the sight in front of me.

Daisy looked over Neal's shoulder, and our eyes met. She was lost in a cloud of love. She pushed up, causing Neal to rub against my member. The sound of flesh slapping against flesh was music to my ears.

Neal captured Daisy's tight nipple in his mouth, and she groaned. "Come for Neal, love." Her eyes rolled back.

"Neal!" Daisy screamed.

It was time to stop watching and join. "Hold

still." I ran my hand down Neal's back and grasped his balls in one of my hands. Neal groaned, and Daisy raised her hips for more friction. I poured lube on Neal's ass and worked my finger around his rim. Memories of Neal's office flashed through my mind, and I remembered his tight ass and how good it felt around my cock.

Neal pushed back as my finger rounded the rim. "Patience." I gently pushed my middle finger inside and worked the lube around. "I need you to relax."

"Hurry. I want you in me. I can't hold on much longer," Neal gritted out. "I need your cock, Aaron."

I lined my dick up with his tight hole and slowly pushed forward. It was so tight and warm, but his muscles fought against me. "Relax, Neal." I had to fight against the orgasm. He felt so good.

He pushed back, taking me at a steady pace. I leaned forward and kissed Daisy over his shoulder.

"Move," Daisy begged. "I'm so close."

Neal pushed back and took all of my dick, and I clenched my eyes closed to last—he was so tight. I wouldn't be able to last long. It was too good.

I gripped Neal's hips and pushed forward. The heat and pressure drove me crazy with each thrust. Neal's hole sucked me in with each push—he felt tighter than the last time we were together. Daisy cried out below Neal. Then Neal pushed forward, grunted, and filled Daisy before slumping forward and kissing her forehead.

My spine tingled, and my balls tightened. I pushed forward and released into Neal. It felt as if my orgasm would never stop. I gave one last push before I slipped out and rolled to the side. The three of us were panting from the lovemaking.

"That was amazing," Daisy gasped. "Can we go again?"

Neal let out a chuckle. "Give us a couple minutes, love."

Daisy crawled between us, and Neal laid his hand over her.

"I love you both," Daisy said. "Is this what the rest of our lives are going to be like?"

I couldn't wait to find out.

Neal's head came up. "We need to do this as much as possible before the babies come."

Daisy and I both let out a chuckle, and we spent the rest of the night making love. Life could not have gotten any better.

12

DAISY

The warm cup of hot chocolate felt good in my cold hands. Two days had passed since I'd heard James's voice and saw Aaron knock him on his ass. It was the best and worst night of my life. Having to relive a part of my past sucked, but the night I spent with Aaron and Neal would hold a place in my heart.

I shifted on the designer couch I'd had my ass plastered to for the last two hours as I watched my men come down the mountain. Annabella decided at the last minute to join us in Denver for Christmas. She never spoke about her past or her soon-to-be husband, and the tabloids had never talked about her family. If she wanted to discuss it, I would listen.

The morning before we left, she came to Aaron's

house. I asked if she wanted to fly to Denver and spend the holidays with us. She immediately said no because she didn't want to intrude on our Christmas. That was when Aaron let out a secret he had been harboring. On Christmas Day, everyone planned to fly in and spend the rest of the week with us.

I couldn't wait for Annabella to meet Jessica, Bridget, and Sophie. I heard Aaron talk about his love of skiing, and I knew Neal had never been before. I told them to go. They didn't want to leave me alone, so when Annabella said she would stay with me while they skied, Aaron and Neal both worked fast to get ready.

I would've loved to have gone with them, but I didn't want to chance a fall. I'd already dealt with enough stress. The ski resort a mile from Aaron's house was breathtaking. Aaron had built his cabin on the mountain that Neal and Aaron skied down. He told me it was a private ski resort, and the owners had given him a plot of land when he bought into it.

I'd seen money when I lived out in Hollywood, and his place wasn't a cabin, even though that's what he called it. When I thought of a cabin, I pictured a one-bedroom log home with a fireplace. His cabin was a six-thousand-square-foot home decked out with all the latest gadgets. The back deck had a hot tub with a view of the valley between the mountains.

If the members didn't want to build a house, they stayed at the state-of-the-art ski lodge that overlooked the mountain trails, and Annabella and I had been in the lodge since the men went out to ski. We sat in front of a warm fire and watched out the window.

Powdery snowflakes fell and made it feel like Christmas. In the corner, a ten-foot Christmas tree was decked out in gold and silver ornaments. It made me think about the tree at our penthouse. I couldn't wait to decorate the tree with my men and kids. *Kids —I still can't believe I'm pregnant with twins.*

Without realizing it, I rubbed my flat stomach.

"Are you excited for the twins?"

"I'm so excited. We still have so much to figure out in our relationship before the twins come. I hope we can sit down and figure everything out after the holidays. I don't know if we'll get married. Whose name do I put on the birth certificate? And how the hell can I stop Aaron from buying every toy he sees online? I'm scared to see what the penthouse will look like when we get back."

That morning, I caught him ordering a set of blankets on Amazon. Neal wasn't helping either— every time he saw something online, he would show it to Aaron, and then Aaron would buy it. Aaron and Neal's Amazon shopping habit was worse than mine.

"At least they want to help. Some men don't care what happens when a woman gets pregnant." Annabella shook her head.

"I love that they want to help, but it's sometimes a little much with those two. But I love them more than anything. Tell me about your soon-to-be husband."

Annabella pulled the fuzzy white blanket off the side of the couch and draped it over her body. "I don't even know where to start."

I took a sip of my hot chocolate. "The beginning would be the best place."

Annabella took a long sip of her wine. Since she wasn't pregnant, she'd ordered a bottle of white wine for herself. "Nate needs me to marry him to help get control of his father's company. I've known him for years. He was there for me when I was younger and dealing with my deadbeat mom. When he asked if I would help, I agreed. There is nothing between Nate and me—he swings for the other team. So I'm doing him a favor."

"Loaning someone money is a favor. Marrying someone so they can acquire a company is next level.

There has to be another way. Let me ask my boss, Brock."

"I appreciate your concern, but you won't change my mind. Now, let's talk about the feast we're going to cook tomorrow for Christmas. Growing up, I had this one foster family that celebrated Christmas with a big dinner, then everyone sat around the tree and opened gifts. It was the best year of my life."

Like Aaron, I was excited for Christmas this year. I couldn't wait. I took the last swig of my hot chocolate. I couldn't believe I drank it that fast, but it was delicious and even had mini marshmallows. "Aaron wanted to have the meal tomorrow catered, but I stopped him. I think between all of us, we can figure out what to cook. I looked in his fridge, and someone already stocked it with everything we need. We don't need a chef. It will be more fun to cook together."

I hoped it would be fun and that we wouldn't end up needing to order pizza because we burned the food. I gazed out the window and watched as the snow came down more heavily. The visibility had decreased. In the corner, a large TV played the weather channel, and a woman was talking about a blizzard on its way toward Denver. I hoped our friends from Ft. Lauderdale would still make it in tomorrow, but if not, I knew the four of us would have fun.

"I agree with the no chef. We got this. It's not as if Aaron doesn't have connections. If need be, someone will come to bail us out, and we won't go hungry." She shook her head. "Those men would never let you go hungry. I'm still surprised Aaron is letting you cook. He's scared everything you do will hurt the babies."

We'd had a long conversation about that two nights before. I wanted my dom, but he worried the babies could get hurt. The three of us came to an understanding. If I thought something would hurt the babies, I would say a safe word. Everything outside the bedroom was purely up to me—I knew what I could and couldn't do safely. "I think Aaron and Neal worry. They'll get better."

Her lips curled into a slight smile. "Those men worship the ground you walk on. They might act like they're lightening up, but they will find a way to make sure you are okay at all times. Damn, I had given up on men until I saw the way Neal and Aaron treat you."

I leaned forward and set the mug on the table. "This is why you shouldn't marry Nate. You will find someone. If you would let me help, I have the perfect man for you. He might not be the sexiest guy in the world, but he would worship the ground you walk on, and that is the most important thing. And he would never be after your money."

"I know looks aren't important. I dated a handsome man, and it was the worst mistake of my life. I need to do this for Nate. I owe him," she said with a sigh, as though the words she spoke were a howl. "When the commitment is over with Nate, I might take you up on your offer."

I couldn't hold back my grin. "I won't bring it up again." It didn't mean I wouldn't try to set her up without knowing. Since I'd met Aaron and Neal, I'd wanted everyone to be happy.

A cold chill crossed my skin, and I looked around the lodge for what caused it. Something seemed off, but maybe it was the lack of hot chocolate in my hands. The waiter must have read my mind because he walked over with a fresh cup, and I took several sips. I gripped it in my hands, and it helped to take the chill out of the air. But something felt wrong.

"Did you see something?" Annabella asked, concerned.

My gut told me something was off, but I didn't know what. My nerves had been on edge since James had gone to jail, but the evil man was behind bars. I knew no one else who would be after me.

I'm overreacting. "I don't know. Something just felt strange." Sudden exhaustion overtook me. "I think I'm getting tired."

Annabella opened then closed her mouth. "Maybe we should head back to the cabin. Neal and Aaron wouldn't be upset if we headed back, especially if you're tired. They would probably be mad if you stayed here while you were sleepy."

"I think I'll head to the bathroom, then we can go." I had consumed four hot chocolates in the past hour, but the damn imported, expensive chocolate was so good. I didn't even want to know what they cost. Aaron said everything went onto his card and not to worry.

Annabella stood to follow me to the bathroom, but I told her I was okay and I could go by myself. The bathroom was on the other side of the lodge. With each step I took, my eyes became more tired. *Damn, maybe Annabella should've come with me.* I wanted to lie down on the floor, curl up in a ball, and take a nap.

My eyelids felt as though someone had put weights on them. I strained to keep my eyes open as I reached the bathroom door. I pulled the door open and spotted a chair inside the room. I needed to sit for a second. My body wouldn't go any farther. I sat in the chair then pulled out my phone to call Annabella and ask her to meet me in the bathroom.

Something wasn't right. I shouldn't have been so tired. It had seemed to hit me as I'd sipped the last hot chocolate. Once I had my phone out, I tried hard to read the contacts, but my eyes wouldn't focus. The last thing I remembered was the door to the bathroom opening before my world went dark.

13

NEAL

I loved the feel of the powdered snow as I raced Aaron down the mountain. I knew he let me win the first time we went down. Aaron had hired a private instructor to teach me the basics before we went down a green trail. I couldn't wait to come out here again and do it with Daisy. At the thought of her name, I looked in the direction of the lodge.

We had done our last run of the day as we skied to the bench to take off our skis.

"You nervous about tomorrow?" I knew Daisy would say yes when we asked her to marry us, but my stomach twisted anyway.

Aaron pulled off his gloves and sat on the bench next to me. "I'm not nervous. If I had a choice, we would fly to Vegas before the new year to make it official."

My phone shrilled in my pocket, and Brock's name flashed on the screen. I closed my eyes and tried to banish the dread. Brock said he would only call if there had been a change in the case.

I glanced in Aaron's direction before I answered the phone. Aaron clenched his jaw, and the same dread went through me before answering. I didn't think the worry would ever go away, or until all the people from Daisy's past were locked up. I swiped across the screen to answer.

"Brock?"

"The FBI searched James's house this morning. They found three women in the basement. If it weren't for Daisy, the women would still be down there." Aaron motioned for me to put the phone on speaker. Brock's voice boomed through the phone. "Damn, Neal. These women were in worse shape than Daisy."

"Are they coming back to Ft. Lauderdale?" Brock and his team had brought Daisy back and made sure she got the treatment she needed.

"I don't know. Daisy called to the dom in me, and I wanted to help her. Don't get me wrong, these women need help, but I don't know if they want my help. They are in the hospital as we speak, and I'm going to sit with them when the detective talks to them."

I didn't know who the women were, but I wanted to make sure they got the help they needed. "You can use our penthouse. I know your place is at the club, and we don't know how much that will affect them. Aaron and I planned to move closer to his parents, anyway. A house came on the market this week we can buy." Brock and Jessica lived in the same building as Club Sanctorum. The club entrance was through locked doors, but Neal didn't want to jeopardize the women. And it was time for the three to move out of the penthouse and into a house.

"Thanks, man. That'll help if they want to come back. We talked about them staying with John, but his house is small." John had served as a Navy SEAL for ten years before he retired and joined Blackwood Security, Brock's mercenary company.

"The women will be in the hospital for another week. I planned to stay here, but the woman in charge of James's house escaped the authorities. I'm going to stay and help them find her. From the video surveillance, Regina Ward was the lady who was in charge of Al's house too."

I had a sudden urge to check on Daisy.

Aaron spoke for the first time. "How is that bitch on the streets? I thought they had sentenced everyone involved with the kidnapping to thirty years. How did she get out early?" From the testimony Daisy had given, Regina had tortured her. I also had an alert set up to notify me when she got out of prison, but I hadn't heard anything.

Brock let out a sigh. "The California prison system is overcrowded, and they released her on good behavior. I'm digging into why I wasn't notified. We need to ask Daisy if she received a call about Regina being released."

I looked in Aaron's direction. *Do we want to tell Daisy about Regina getting out?* Aaron was lost in thought. Maybe we could reach out to her therapist and figure out the best way to let her know the woman was back on the streets. "Have you pulled the surveillance around the house?"

Brock huffed. "Yes, Neal, that was the first thing I did. She left this morning, and the FBI raided this afternoon. If she tried to return, she turned around and left. I tracked her car to an office building this morning. The car is there, but she is nowhere in the vicinity." He let out a sigh. "Jessica is flying into Denver tomorrow. She will stay with you until I can get there." Jessica was Brock's very pregnant fiancée. She was also the CFO for my older brother's company, Ross Enterprises. But more than anything, she was one of Daisy's closest friends. They needed to tell Daisy that night about Regina. She would ask questions if Jessica showed up and Brock was still in California.

"Aaron and I finished skiing for the day and are heading into the lounge to pick up Annabella and Daisy. When I get back to the cabin, I can help you look for information. Aaron will call the real estate lawyer and purchase the house." When Aaron shifted, I looked in his direction, and his cheeks had blushed. Seemed our dom was holding on to a secret.

"Keep your eye out in case for some crazy reason she found you guys. I have to go. The lead detective is heading my way."

"Bye."

I turned to Aaron. "You already bought the house, didn't you?" It would be the only reason for him to have squirmed when I mentioned buying it.

He shrugged. "I thought it would be easier to move us when we weren't home. I purchased it before we left, and the movers are moving everything in. But what I'm worried about is Daisy. Do you think that crazy bitch, Regina, knows where we are?

Should I call and have my brother and his partner fly out tonight?" Aaron's brother Asher owned a mercenary company with his twin, Antonio. Asher was engaged to CJ. All were supposed to arrive the next day for a big Christmas Eve dinner.

"No, I don't think she could've made it to Denver already. If she flew, Brock would've caught it when he did his initial search."

Aaron leaned over and wrapped his arms around me. "Let's go get our woman and get her home."

The blast of warm air felt good as we opened the heavy wooden door. Since the lounge was for owners only, it wasn't crowded. But the place was amazing. The chandeliers were crystal, and rich oak ran throughout. When we entered the main area, I spotted Annabella on a plush white couch in front of the fire.

I gazed around the room, looking for Daisy, but I didn't spot her. Aaron was in step with me as we made it over to where Annabella sat. Her eyes gazed at the fire. She hadn't heard us walk up to her.

"Annabella?"

She jumped in her seat and pressed her hand to her chest. "You scared the crap out of me."

I took the seat next to her, and Aaron sat in the matching white chair. "Where's Daisy?"

"Oh, you didn't see her? She just went to the bathroom."

"How are you enjoying the lodge? You sure you don't want your future husband to come and spend some time with you?"

Annabella took a big swig of wine. "It's complicated. I hope you don't mind me spending the holidays with you. If I'm a burden, I can stay here at the lodge or catch a flight back."

Daisy would have been upset if Annabella left. I also wanted her around for when we broke the news to Daisy that the crazy bitch from her nightmares was out of prison. We spent the next ten minutes talking about Christmas Day. Annabella was excited to meet everyone flying in.

But the longer Daisy was gone, the more I worried. *She should be back by now.* "I'm going to go make sure Daisy is okay."

Aaron nodded, and I headed down the hall. I opened the frosted-glass door a sliver. "Daisy, are you in there?" When she didn't respond, I became more concerned. "Is anyone in there?" When no one replied, I opened the door and stepped inside. My stomach clenched when I saw Daisy's white purse, its contents spread across the bathroom floor. Her pink iPhone lay next to the purse. I pushed the door to each stall open and called her name. She wasn't there.

Did the bitch from California have her? I dialed Aaron's phone. "Someone took Daisy," I said when he answered.

14

AARON

I couldn't help but pace outside the bathroom. The detective was inside, and it seemed like an hour had passed since Neal called to let him know that Daisy had disappeared. If anything happened to her, I felt as though my world would crumble. She completed the three of us. I felt helpless. Neal sat in a nearby chair, his fingers working the keyboard.

Numbly, I plopped into the chair next to him.

Neal looked up from his keyboard with a grim look. "Someone cut the video feed to the building. The person who took her knew what they were doing. This system has a state-of-the-art firewall. The other possibility is they knew someone who works here."

I ground my teeth. "The price to live here is high,

and it would cost a lot to pay someone off." Taking a deep breath did nothing to get my mind under control. I wanted to punch the wall.

"Here." Annabella handed me a glass of water. "It might help."

I glanced around the room. The lodge guests huddled behind the tape, trying to get a look. I glared at the property manager as he gawked with the other patrons. He must have realized I wasn't happy, so he had the people move back into the main area. They couldn't leave until the police had questioned them.

"Thanks," I muttered before I took a sip of the water.

"I'm sorry," Annabella whispered. She had tears running down her face. "I should've gone with her. I didn't know she was still in danger."

There was no doubt in my mind that Annabella felt bad. I stood up and pulled her into my arms. She started to cry harder. "I just... got her... back." She sobbed into my shirt.

"We will find her." I wouldn't stop until we did.

When Annabella stopped crying, I guided her into the seat next to me.

"You think Regina did this?" I asked Neal.

"Brock ran her face through the video feed of the airport. Nothing came back. We've also sent her picture through the video feed of the street cameras. It's as if she is still in that same building or she somehow went through a tunnel. The police are researching the building she went into."

"Why would this woman want her?" Annabella asked.

Neal ran his hand through his hair. "People go crazy when they are at the end of their rope. The prison released her because of overcrowding. But she did the same thing again. She helped keep three women as prisoners, and there is no way a judge won't give her life in prison. The pictures I saw of these women are bad." Neal shook his head. "Regina has nothing left to live for except the need for revenge against Daisy."

The bathroom door opened, and the detective stepped out with evidence bags. Each bag held pieces of Daisy's things.

The silver locket in one bag caught my eye—it had her tracker in it. When she first moved to Ft. Lauderdale, she would wander off, and Brock got worried, so he had a necklace made to help track her location. I'd asked her why she still wore it, and she'd said it felt like a security blanket. Now, her security blanket sat in an evidence bag.

I squinted to look closer and saw that the chain to the necklace was broken. "Hey, Neal."

He raised his head from the computer.

"Come here."

In a few short strides, he was next to me.

I pointed to the evidence bag. "Whoever took Daisy ripped her necklace off. How would Regina know about her tracker?"

The detective looked down at the bag. "She probably didn't want you to track her if she left you."

My day job was a movie star, but I had done hours of research for each role. In one movie, I played a detective, and I'd spent six weeks following a cop around and learning all aspects of the job. "She wouldn't leave us." Neal shook his head next to me.

The guy looked back at the door. "Personally, I think it's nothing more than a woman who changed her mind and no longer wants to be with you. She dropped her purse before she left."

"That doesn't even sound right. Why would she leave her purse and her money if she wanted to escape us?"

The detective didn't seem to care. He glanced down at his watch. "I'll take the evidence to the sheriff's office and let the next shift know your girlfriend is missing. You can't file a missing person's report for twenty-four hours."

"You've got to be fucking kidding me. Someone kidnapped her."

The detective glanced at his watch again. "In my professional opinion, it looks like she dropped her purse before she left. There are no signs of a struggle."

I glanced at Neal, and his eyes looked past the detective. "Can I see the pictures of the crime scene?" Neal's voice sounded deadly.

The detective shrugged. "I didn't think they were necessary. We picked up her stuff and put it in a bag. She can come down to the station. She probably just got sick of you." He tapped his watch. "My shift is over. You can talk to the detective on the shift after mine."

He turned and left. I couldn't believe what I'd heard. "Did I hear that conversation correctly? I want the number to the chief of police. I will have his badge by the end of the day."

Neal hugged me. "We don't need the police to find Daisy. We will get her back ourselves. I need to look into him." He pulled back. "There's something off about him. He couldn't wait to get out of this building. I overheard that he sent the other detective home and said he could handle the scene. Let's get home so I have all my computers and can find her. We will find her."

Anger from the cop blowing us off still bubbled under the surface. I wasn't used to people not doing what I told them to do, but Neal was right. I had faith he would be able to track Daisy down. I couldn't think something would happen to her.

"Let's head to the house," he said, "and I will put up a comm between us and Brock. As for that guy, I will take care of him after we find our woman."

Neal

The detective's background came back clean. He had a wife and kids and never so much as a parking ticket. He volunteered for every event at his daughter's school. Pictures online suggested that he took good care of his wife.

The next thing to do was get back to searching for Regina. Everything led to her—she never left the building. I watched the footage over and over. She walked into a building in downtown LA and never came out. Ten men walked into the office building and never came out. Brock and I had both gone through the video feed. I looked for signs someone had faked it.

Brock's face came across the screen. Aaron drew his brows together. "We found Regina. The building has a secret room. The FBI missed their first sweep. When they raided the room, they walked into a sex-slave trade. Sixteen women were up for sale, and those ten men were there to buy them. Regina was in charge of the sale."

"Fuck," I mumbled.

"Yep, this means she isn't part of Daisy's kidnapping. I know no one who would want to kidnap her. Did she make anyone mad in LA?"

I thought back to the party. Daisy barely had time to see anyone before we left. "Do you think it could be one of Aaron's crazy fans? The detective at the scene today brushed us off and would barely investigate the case. The first person I researched was the detective, and his past came back clean. No ties to anyone in Daisy's past."

"But we were both outed," Aaron said. "Why take her and not us?"

"Maybe it was someone who saw her on TV and wanted her to be his. Is there another man still planning his revenge on Daisy? Is James still in jail? I hadn't thought to check him," Brock said.

I pinched the bridge of my nose. "Since we know it's not Regina, are you heading to Denver? More people here to help find her would be nice."

Aaron left the room, and Brock let out a sigh. "Yeah, I plan to be there in few hours. I'd hoped it was Regina. I hate not knowing who has her."

"See you in a few."

"Bye."

I didn't need to look to know that Aaron had stepped back into the study that I had taken over since we arrived at the cabin. Annabella was in the kitchen, preparing for our family and friends who boarded a plane the second we told them Daisy was missing.

He set a plate down and squeezed my shoulder. "You need to eat."

"I don't have an appetite. I keep looking through the video of the premiere and the security footage here before someone cut the video, but I see nothing."

Aaron grabbed the chair from the other side and dragged it around the desk. He reached over and squeezed my hand.

"Let me look with you." He nodded toward the phone. "Did Brock discover any information on Regina?"

I leaned back in the cushy chair and explained what the police had found and the women they ended up saving. Daisy going back to California was both the worst and best idea. Her presence had helped save tons of women but at the cost of the girl I loved. Aaron let out a whistle when I finished telling him about the women the police saved from the auction and that they had arrested ten men. I knew when they searched those men's houses, they would find more women.

I hoped the women would be able to live normal lives. It has taken Daisy years to come back from the way Al had treated her, and she still wasn't close to mentally healing all the way.

Aaron leaned forward in the chair next to mine. "Pull up the feed. I was so busy checking you and Daisy out that I didn't pay attention to the crowd. Let's see if someone looked off."

Brock had collected a feed from the police at the premiere. I had also hacked the security cameras of the movie theaters.

"Damn, Daisy looked hot in that dress," Aaron grumbled as I fast-forwarded through the video. "Stop!" Aaron yelled. "Go back a few seconds."

Aaron pointed to an overweight man wearing a

tux and standing behind the paparazzi. "He shouldn't have been there."

The man looked familiar, and I remembered where I'd seen him before. I opened another video file of the lodge. I played the video. "He was at the lodge. Do you know who that is?"

"Yes. Call Brock. I know who has our woman."

15

NEAL

Once Antonio, Asher, and Brock arrived, we jumped into Aaron's SUV and headed toward the GPS location I'd pinned down from satellite imagery. The blue dot seemed so far away. I had no doubt that the men in the SUV would rescue Daisy, but that didn't mean I planned to wait at the cabin for them. Once I knew who I was looking for, it only took a matter of minutes to find the fucker's location. Waiting for Antonio and Brock to show up was the long part.

When Antonio turned onto the main highway, he pushed down on the accelerator. No matter how fast he went, the GPS dot felt miles away. Aaron pressed his hand to my knee to stop my nervous twitch. I hadn't even realized it had been bouncing.

Every minute it took to get her back was another minute the crazy fucker had to terrify Daisy, and she had dealt with enough crazy people in her past.

"Everyone knows the plan, right?" Antonio asked. Everyone in the SUV answered in the affirmative.

Antonio finally turned onto the gravel road toward the cabin Daisy was being held in. We donned night-vision goggles to aid in a surprise attack. When Antonio turned off the headlights and continued down the road at an aggressive rate, I gripped the oh-shit handle. He slowed the SUV a quarter mile from the cabin then angled it to block the road. Before he shifted into Park, Aaron and I jumped out.

"Neal, you go with Brock. Aaron, you go with Asher and me," Antonio's voice was low and serious. "Remember that we don't know exactly what we're dealing with. He could have someone helping him, and he's unhinged. Keep your eyes open. Understand?"

We'd planned for one team to breach the front and the other team to enter through the back. Brock and I headed for the back of the house. The night-vision goggles made the trek through the high brush and trees easier. Brock had handed me a gun when we left the house. I'd put it in a holster and hoped I wouldn't need to use it. I wanted Harry, Aaron's ex-agent, to pay for what he did, and a quick death would be too easy.

I'd downloaded a floor plan off the internet, and both Antonio and Brock seemed to think Harry held her in the study. I would do anything Antonio asked as long as we got Daisy back. After this kidnapping, I wanted to plant a tracking device in her arm. I didn't care how creepy that sounded. I never wanted to experience the feeling of losing her again.

"The house should be coming into view about a thousand feet ahead," Antonio said through the comm. Asher had come with a plane full of tackle gear, including comms for us to hear each other as we made our way to the house.

I could feel the adrenaline coursing through my veins, and all I wanted to do was get my woman back. I would never let her out of my sight again. I didn't know what I would do if Daisy died. Aaron and I both needed her. She made us complete. She was relying on us to make sure we got her out of this cabin safety, and I didn't plan to let her down.

We were within a hundred feet of the house. The woods had become deadly quiet—the only sound was an owl off in the distance. Brock moved swiftly in front of me and cleared a path through the tall grass in the forest.

I still couldn't comprehend how or why Aaron's agent had kidnapped her. Yes, Aaron had made him a lot of money over the years, but now he would spend his time in jail. I wondered what he thought kidnapping Daisy would get him. Aaron would never work for him again.

Antonio's voice came over the comm. "It's go time."

Daisy

"Wake up, bitch." I was already awake. Then I felt ice-cold water on me. When I awoke, I felt my hands bound to a chair. During my years spent with Al, I'd crafted the act of pretending to sleep. It might have been years ago, but I still remembered how to pretend to be asleep.

I slowly opened my eyes to take in where I was and what had happened. The last thing I remembered was going into the bathroom, and my world went black. I had let my guard down. I'd thought nobody would come after me in Denver. *How could someone have known we were there?*

When I glanced around the room and ignored the overweight asshole in front of me, I noticed we were in a cabin, and it looked like the same trees that surrounded Aaron's cabin. I let out a sigh. At least I was still in Colorado. Hopefully, Aaron and Neal would find me. I glanced down and noticed they'd taken my necklace. *Fuck.*

"You think I would have left that necklace on you? I know Aaron's a control freak and needs to know where you are at all times. But I want to play with you before I let him know I have you."

Aaron wasn't a control freak. I wanted the necklace. It made me feel secure. I did learn one thing though: the fucker knew Aaron, so he wasn't someone from my horrible past. That made it a little easier. "If you want money, I can get it for you. Tell me what you want. Money, drugs? I can get it for you."

My main goal was to keep him talking and bide my time. I knew my men would find me, and I knew Brock would work at it too. The crazy man paced in front of my chair. As I followed him back and forth with my eyes, I noticed another man in the corner. He hadn't said a word since I'd awoken.

"Don't look at him." The big man nodded toward

the man in the corner. "He won't help you. I've made sure of that."

"I don't understand what you want from me."

"I want to see Aaron suffer, and you are my key to that." His whiny voice hit a new octave that hurt my eardrums.

I worked to remember everyone Aaron had introduced me to in Hollywood a couple days before. This man didn't look familiar—I hadn't seen him at all. "Whatever Aaron did, we can fix it, I promise."

The crazy guy stopped pacing and trained his bloodshot eyes on me. "He ruined everything and for what? A piece of ass. That is all you are."

"I don't understand how I ruined everything."

He grunted. "He left the industry for you."

Everything seemed to click into place. "You're his agent." I nodded to the guy in the corner. "Who is he?"

"I was his agent until you came around and put new ideas in his head." He waved his hand in the other direction. "He helped me get you. The detective was on your case. He made your men believe you ran away. When this is over, I will tell him where he can find his family. But in case Aaron gets some idea to come after you, I have a backup plan."

"Bullshit!" I screamed. "There's no way Aaron

and Neal believe I ran away." I was livid at the fucker who had tried to trick my men. "Aaron and Neal would never believe you. I bet they're still looking for me."

The detective in the corner raised his head "I'm sorry, ma'am," he said, his eyes downcast. "I need my family back. I told them it looked like you ran away and they would have to wait twenty-four hours to make a statement. Your friends left and said they would wait until tomorrow."

"See? They don't care about you that much." My kidnapper sneered at me.

"So, what's your plan? Keep me here until Aaron decides to work for you again?"

"His chance to work in the industry is over!" the fucker yelled. "I want him to pay for making me look like an idiot." The man wasn't rational. He wiped his hand across his nose.

"How did Aaron make you look like an idiot?" I really didn't care what his answer would be. I needed him distracted so I could continue to work my arms back and forth in the ropes—I needed to wiggle out of them. It would be my only chance. I knew my men wouldn't have given up and walked out.

"I had promised he would do the next movie for Carwel, and the next day, he announced he was retiring. He left millions on the table. What am I going to do now? I owe people money, and Aaron's next film would have set me up for a long time. Now they are coming for me."

I sighed. "Let me get this straight. You promised Aaron would do a movie before you spoke to him because you needed the payday. The reason you needed the payday was that you snorted all your money up your nose, and now you have no way to pay your drug dealer. How could you not have money? Aaron has made millions over the years, and you've been his agent. Using Aaron to support your drug habit sure makes you look like an idiot."

For a crazy, old, fat fucker, he could move. Being tied to the chair didn't give me the chance to get out of the way before his fist came across my face. The pain radiated through my body. It hurt like a bitch, and I couldn't stop the tears that leaked from my eyes. Blood poured from my nose, but it didn't feel broken. Al had broken my nose a couple of times, so I knew what it sounded and felt like. Nope, that was one good thing. I didn't have to go through the pain of getting it set.

"You will pay for that," the fat fucker said. "I know what you used to do for Al. Aaron sat and bragged about this woman he fell for, telling me all about how he planned to leave the industry for you. You are nothing but a whore. I'm going to have fun with you."

"Hey, man, that's not what we agreed to," the detective said. "You said this guy owed you money and, once you got what you wanted, we would let her go and you would tell me where my family is."

I felt bad for the dumbass detective. If anyone kidnapped Neal or Aaron, I would do anything to get them back. But I would also understand that a crazy person would never give me what I wanted. He should've gone to his supervisor and let them know what was going on.

Aaron's ex-agent pulled a gun out of his waistband and turned toward the detective. I used that opportunity to work on the ropes.

"You listen here, you idiot," my captor said in a low voice. "I will put a bullet through your head if I hear you whine one more time."

Harry and the detective stared at each other for a minute before the detective grumbled, "I understand."

"I'm not sure you do," Harry replied, "but this might help." I saw his finger squeeze the trigger. He shot the detective in the leg. "Now, it's time to have some fun with Aaron's whore."

"Please don't hurt me," I said. "I can make sure Aaron doesn't quit Hollywood."

"There is no way Aaron won't turn me in after this. Time for some fun."

He took two quick strides my way, then he pulled the ropes from around my wrists. When he had me untied, he pointed the gun at my head. "Walk," he barked.

He pushed me toward the back of the house. We took a couple of steps into the room, then he shoved me from behind, and I fell onto the bed. He continued to point the gun at me.

"I can't wait to make you mine. Then every time Aaron looks at you, he'll know I've had you."

Aaron

Antonio crouched a hundred feet from the cabin. We could see Harry pacing through the window. The night-vision goggles picked up another individual in the living room. There were three people in the back of the house huddled together. Daisy sat in a chair. I wanted to rush in and grab her but knew I had to wait for Antonio's call.

I couldn't hear what Harry said to Daisy, but he

looked angrier with each word. I didn't think it would be long before he lost his cool. And it wasn't—he swung and punched Daisy in the face.

Asher's hand grabbed my arm. "Keep your cool, man. Daisy's strong, and we will get her back. If we don't do this correctly, someone will get hurt. Trust me, brother, it kills me to see her get punched, but we need to keep level heads."

"How much longer?" I asked. I didn't know if I could handle watching her get hit again.

Something got Harry's attention. He turned toward the other person in the room, and the sound of gunfire startled me. "So, help me, Antonio, if we don't go in now, I will go in alone and kill the fucker."

And with that, he motioned for everyone to breach the house.

Brock and Neal entered the back door. When they were inside, Brock notified us over the comm. As we walked toward the front door, Harry grabbed Daisy and dragged her out of the room. Her screams pierced my heart.

We entered the house to find the detective, with blood coming out of a bullet wound, sitting in a chair to the side. Anger coursed through me—the fucker had helped this nutjob kidnap my woman then tried to play it off as if she didn't want to be with us.

It didn't take long to cross the room. "Why?" I asked.

"He has my fam—" He lost consciousness.

Asher reached for his belt and tied it around the detective's leg. Brock's voice came over the comm. "One woman and two kids. They are out, and I can't wake them." Harry must have drugged them.

Screams from the bedroom had me rushing toward Daisy's voice.

I looked around. Harry had a gun pointed at Daisy's head. He had ripped her pants off, and his zipper was down.

"Put down the gun," Antonio ordered. "It's over, Harry."

"I have nothing left to live for. If you don't kill me, my drug dealer will," Harry said. "Back off, or I will kill her."

"Put the gun down. We can talk about this. If it's money you need, I will give it to you." He swung his head in my direction.

"Fuck off. You had your chance. Now, I'm going to take something you love away. Why did you have to quit? You ruined everything."

"Stop this before someone dies and you go to

prison for life. The detective might live, but we need to get him help."

Brock's voice came over the comm to let us know the police and an ambulance were five minutes out.

"Listen to Aaron," Brock said. "Set the gun down and wait for the police."

"I'm not stupid," Harry said. "The police are already on the way. I won't go to jail again." He swung the gun in my direction. "Everything is about Aaron, it's time he learns he doesn't always get his way."

Daisy used that moment to spring into action. When Harry pointed the gun at me, she brought her elbow down into his gut. I hadn't noticed Asher make his way over to the side of the bed, but he grabbed Daisy, swung her to the ground, and covered her.

"Fuck you!" Harry screamed, as he pointed the gun at Daisy and pulled the trigger.

Antonio launched his body at Harry. Harry let out a grunt as Antonio hit him with force.

I rushed to Asher and Daisy and felt helpless as the blood ran from my brother's side. Daisy moved over. "Help him," she said. I pressed my hands to the side of my brother's chest.

Asher's eyes fluttered open as I held pressure on

his wound. "Come on, Asher. Stay with me. The ambulance is two minutes out."

Harry kept yelling in the background as Antonio subdued him. I didn't see what Antonio did, but I could hear the grunts as he landed a few punches into Harry's side. I wanted to kick the shit out of him, but my hands were busy applying pressure to my brother's wound. Daisy put Asher's head in her lap and whispered to him, telling him he needed to stay strong, or CJ, Asher's fiancée, would be mad.

"Brock, how far out is the ambulance?" I yelled as Asher's eyes kept closing. "He's losing blood fast."

"Aaron, tell CJ I will be okay," Asher said urgently. "He'll worry."

"Don't worry about anything except staying alive."

I didn't know if he heard me before his eyes shut and his breathing became labored. Luckily, the EMTs rushed through the door.

16

DAISY

I shot straight up in bed. I glanced around the room and let out a breath, my heart pounding out of my chest. I'd dreamt I was in Al's dungeon.

"What's wrong?" Neal pulled me into his arms, and Aaron slowly sat up next to me. We hadn't arrived back to the cabin until around midnight, and then I'd sat up with Jessica and Bridget while the men went to the hospital. Asher was going to be okay. The bullet missed major organs, and they planned to release him that morning.

"Sorry." I tried to calm my nerves. "I dreamt I was back in Al's house." Neal's arms tightened around me.

"No one will ever take you away from us again. When we get back, I'm going to put a GPS device in your arm. I don't care if you think I'm crazy. I never want to go through not knowing where you are again."

"I would like that." I had nothing to hide, and Aaron and Neal wouldn't abuse the tracker. Being kidnapped three times in my life was enough.

I screamed again as the door thrust open. Bridget gazed around the room, her face going from excited to irritated at finding us awake in bed.

"Go away, Bridget!" I said as Neal tried to hide beneath the covers. Dang.

She tapped her green, bell-accessorized slippers on the floor. She was wearing elf PJs and elf ears. "Not a chance. Ant and Alonzo woke up an hour ago," Bridget said. "It's Christmas morning, and I want to open my presents." A mischievous smile crossed her face as she continued to tap her shoe on the floor.

"Can't we sleep for another hour? We were all up late," Neal pointed out.

"My son doesn't seem to understand that we were up late, and I want to open my presents. Jessica has breakfast on the table, and if you plan on eating, you'd better hurry before the men downstairs eat all the food." Those were her parting words before she turned on her heel and exited the bedroom.

"What time is it? I feel like we just went to bed."

I pulled myself out of Neal's arms and rolled over to Aaron. "You're the one who loves Christmas. Don't you want to watch your nephew open the gifts we bought him?" I had found every noisy gift possible for Alonzo, and I couldn't wait to watch him make a racket. I had done the same thing for Ant.

"You're right that I want to watch them, but I'm tempted to stay in bed with you." Aaron leaned in and captured my lips.

Neal leaned over my back and kissed his way up my neck. I was lost in the sensation when the door to our bedroom flew open again. Neal kissed my neck one more time before he leaned back. We confronted a new intruder.

"Uncles and Auntie, I want to open gifts." Ant wore Christmas PJs that matched Jessica's.

"Okay, buddy, we will be down in a few. Can you shut the door, and we will come down?"

Once our little intruder left, Aaron threw off the covers, yanked on a pair of sweats he'd discarded nearby, and rose from the bed.

I couldn't help but stare at his naked backside. I wasn't the only one. Neal watched with his mouth dropped open. Damn, he was sexy. His sweatpants rode low on his amazing hips, showing his back muscles, and if he turned around, I would see the sexy abs I enjoyed running my hands all over.

Aaron turned around, and I gazed at his perfect abs and licked my lips. I wanted to run my mouth all over him. "Are you two going to lie in bed and stare or get ready?" Aaron asked with a mischievous grin. He knew exactly what was going through my mind. If a cute six-year-old hadn't been waiting for us downstairs, I would have made love to my men.

"Fine. I'm getting up," Neal grumbled, and I saw another sexy backside. I was the luckiest woman on the planet.

"I hope your brother gets out so we can open gifts," I said.

Aaron walked over to the door and flipped the lock. "Or we can ignore the outside world and head back to bed."

"It's enticing..." And I actually considered it for a second. But the pitter-patter of little feet outside the door changed my mind. "Nope. Let's celebrate the holiday with our friends, then you guys can come back up here and unwrap me," I said. I dodged Aaron's arm as he reached for me and ran to the bathroom.

The second I shut the door, I flipped the lock, knowing that they would try to follow me. The shower felt good. When I came out, Aaron grabbed me around the waist and lifted me into his arms. "You are the most beautiful woman alive."

"We have to go downstairs," I reminded him. I tried to say it sternly, but giggles bubbled from me. "Your nephew will be back soon if we don't go downstairs."

Aaron leaned in and gave me a deep kiss. Before I had time to head to the door, Neal pulled me in. My body was on fire. Neal broke me from my daze. "Let's go down."

When we opened the door, an angry six-year-old stood in wait. "Come on, Uncle Aaron and Uncle Neal. I want to open gifts."

Aaron reached down, swooped Ant into his arms, and tickled his sides. "Let's go see what's under the tree."

Ant's laughter brought a smile to my face. It was going to be the best Christmas ever, and the day had just started. I followed my two men down the stairs.

I couldn't help but stop halfway down, just as the living room was in sight. Aaron's entire family sat around the living room with our friends. Brock sat in a chair with Jessica in his lap. Alonzo crawled around on the floor. Sophie and Zane sat on the floor next to him. But I never expected to see the president of the United States in the house. Zack sat on the chair, sipping a cup of coffee and smiling at the people in the room.

A huge tree stood in the middle, and it looked like a department store. I hadn't seen the gifts last night when we came home. I was so tired that I didn't pay attention. There were so many presents that they didn't fit under the tree.

The three of us cuddled together on the love seat. It didn't take long for laughter to fill the cabin, with the sound of paper tearing under the chuckles. I was enjoying watching everyone opening gifts. I hadn't even opened any of mine when Ant walked up with a small box and handed it to me. "Here, Auntie Daisy. This one is for you." I leaned over, grabbed the gift, and gave him a kiss on the cheek before he ran back to his parents.

I tried to hold back the emotions of the day. My damn hormones had me on the verge of tears all morning. I slowly pulled off the wrapping paper, savoring the first Christmas present from my men. Aaron had scribbled his and Neal's name on the top. It meant more that he put their names on it instead of allowing the gift wrapper at the store to write the card. They both had opened their gifts—I had given each of them a framed ultrasound photo of their babies. After I pulled the last piece of paper away, a ring box sat in my hands. My hand shook as I opened the top. I gasped at the pink diamond ring inside. I could barely see it through the tears running down my face.

I turned to Neal, who was down on one knee. Aaron sat next to me and grabbed my hand. I glanced back at Neal, and he had so much love in his eyes. Ant stood next to him and couldn't help but smile.

"Daisy, this past year we have been through a lot," Neal said. "I know one thing. You make me happy, and when we found Aaron, everything clicked for us. I wanted to ask you in front of our family and friends because these are the people who love you as much as I do. There isn't a day that goes by when I don't want you to be my wife, my partner, and the mother of my children. I'm not sure our lives will be all roses, but I will fight for you with each breath I take to make sure you are happy. Please marry me and make me the happiest man alive."

Neal's eyes bored into me, but how could I say yes to only one? Would Aaron think I didn't love him as much as Neal? I wanted them both to be my husband. When I looked in Aaron's direction, he gave me a smile. "Love, are you going to answer Neal or leave him out to dry?"

I wiped the tears from my face. "I want to say yes, but I also want to marry you. How come I can't marry both of you?"

Aaron wrapped an arm around me. "Love, we might not get married by the government standard, but you will be my wife. And as soon as you say yes to Neal, I can give you my gifts."

"I love you, too, Neal," I whispered. And my voice wobbled between sobs of happiness. "I love you both so much. It would make me the happiest woman alive to be your wife."

"Is that a yes?"

"Yes," I told him.

He picked me up from the couch and swung me around. The living room erupted in congratulations and hugs.

"I still have two more gifts."

Neal pulled me into his lap as we sat back down on the couch. Aaron handed Neal and me another package each. We both slowly worked to pull the paper off. Neal had his open before me, and I heard a gasp come from him.

Aaron got down on one knee. "You both mean the world to me. I don't know what I would do without either of you. Neal, I know we interlocked our finances, so we can never split. But will you wear this collar? It's a necklace to symbolize our love and that I'm your dom."

Neal moved me to the side, and he kissed Aaron. "Yes," he whispered.

I finished opening mine, and inside was a diamond necklace that matched my ring. I didn't give Aaron time to ask—I threw myself into his arms and said yes. The peanut gallery around us let out a laugh, but I didn't care. I had the two most important people in my life next to me on Christmas. I never would have known, five years ago when I almost called it quits on life, that I would end up with the two best men.

Love had found me after all these years, and I wasn't about to let it go.

EPILOGUE - DAISY

One month later

"You did an amazing job today, love." Aaron wrapped me in his arms.

Neal was still sitting at a table full of women. The new Ross Women's Shelter in California opened that day. Aaron had originally wanted to sell his home in California and never look back, but after we got back from Denver, Kat and I sat down and talked about the women's shelter.

The center was to house five of the women from the sex-slave sale the FBI broke up. A few of the women went back to their families, and a few were still in the hospital. One of the women at James's house had been held for eight years. My heart went out to her.

A couple of the women had been kidnapped from Germany, and they both flew home last week.

"I thought Annabella was supposed to be here," Aaron said.

I glanced around the room. "She was. I don't know why she hasn't called yet."

Neal walked over and engulfed me in a hug. "I can't believe you set this up in a month."

I laughed. "I couldn't have done it without you guys. The money you put into the foundation and having the cash to buy a building made things a lot easier."

"You sure you're okay here?"

I rolled my eyes at my protective dom. "Aaron, we've been here for a week. I'm fine. It gets easier each day, and if I have a problem, I can call Dr. Robison."

Neal and Bridget talked over Christmas, and they decided to combine the two cybersecurity companies together. With Bridget back in Ft. Lauderdale, we decided to stay in LA for a month. Aaron and Neal were worried someone would still come after me, so Aaron brought John, one of Brock's mercenaries, along with us.

John had served as a Navy SEAL for ten years before he retired and joined Blackwood Security,

Brock's mercenary company. The military had discharged him when his Humvee ran over an IUD. John had spent months in the hospital from a brain aneurysm and a slice down the side of his face.

I hated how he let the scar on his face define him. He was like a giant teddy bear I wanted to protect.

My phone vibrated in my pocket. Annabella's name flashed across the screen. Since Christmas, we had talked on the phone each day. It was nice to have my friend back, which was why I was surprised she hadn't shown up. "Where are you?" I asked.

"I need help. I was arrested for murdering Nate." Annabella's voice shook.

THE END – UNTIL ANNABELLA'S AND JOHN'S STORY!

AUTHOR'S NOTE

White Hat Security Series

Hacker Exposed
    Royal Hacker
    Misunderstood Hacker
    Undercover Hacker
    Hacker Revelation
    Hacker Christmas

Montana Gold (Brotherhood Kindle World)

    Grayson's Angel
    Noah's Love
    Bryson's Treasure - 2019

A Flipping Love Story (Badge of Honor World)

Unlocking Dreams
Unlocking Hope - 2019

Visit linzibaxter.com for more information and release dates.
Join Linzi Baxter Newsletter at Newsletter

ABOUT AUTHOR

Linzi Baxter lives in Orlando, Florida with her husband and lazy basset hound. She started writing when voices inside her head wouldn't stop talking until the story was told. When not at work as an IT Manager, Linzi enjoys writing action-packed romances that will take you to the edge of your seat.

She enjoys engaging her readers with strong, interesting characters that have complex and stimulating stories to tell. If you enjoy a little (or maybe a whole lot) of steam and spice, don't miss checking out White Hat Security series.

When not writing, Linzi enjoys reading, watching college sports (GO UCF Knights), and traveling to Europe. She loves hearing from her readers and can't wait to hear from you!

Made in the USA
Monee, IL
14 January 2020